FIRE AND ICE

LOCUST POINT MYSTERY SERIES, BOOK 10

LIBBY HOWARD

CHAPTER 1

"Welcome to Foxdancer Lodge!"

The man greeted us with the booming voice of someone announcing circus performers. His dark hair was slicked back from a tanned and weathered face that appeared old enough to have had a little salt mixed in with the pepper. He was wearing dark-wash blue jeans, a light green shirt with mother of pearl buttons, and cowboy boots that looked as if they'd just come out of a box. Blue eyes danced with jolly humor as he smiled widely at us, gesturing for one of the porters to unload our bags from our vehicle.

We'd flown into the airport in Aspen, rented an SUV, and driven the short distance to a little town called Crow Creek. Both the town and the lodge were a quick drive to all the bigger ski resorts. According to the brochures we'd poured over for weeks before we left, Foxdancer Lodge exuded a cozy intimacy that the larger resorts lacked. The town seemed too good to be true from the marketing literature—wholesome and sleepy with a colorful history and dozens of boutique craft and artisan shops.

In addition to the main lodge, there were several cabins

scattered around the edge of the parking lot. Behind the line of buildings was a small terrain park as well as a chair lift that led up to what the literature said were six trails—some groomed and some more suitable for cross-country skiing. Judge Beck had booked us into a suite in the main lodge. Our suite had a private hot tub on the deck outside the common area, overlooking the activities on the terrain park. I knew the kids were eager to hit the slopes, but I was looking forward to unpacking and checking out the accommodations. Yes, we were here to ski and snowboard, but I hoped to get in a few other, less physically taxing, activities on this vacation as well.

"I'm Rocky Forrest." The man who'd greeted us spread his arms wide. "I'm the owner and manager. Let's get you folks checked in and get you out there on the snow."

The kids went ahead with Rocky into the main lodge while the judge and I waited for the porters. We made our way to the front desk while Madison and Henry stared out the huge two-story glass windows that revealed a scene straight from a snow globe.

"The chair lift operator is on duty from seven in the morning until noon, then again from four in the evening until six—or seven if we're busy," Rocky told me as Judge Beck dealt with the checking-in process. "There's a J-bar lift you can turn on if you want to go up on off hours, or you can just ask here at the front desk, and we'll send someone out to fire up the chair lift for you."

From the number of folks lined up at the lift, it looked like many people took advantage of the ski trails as well as the terrain park. "Are the slopes just for lodge guests, or do locals use them as well?" I wondered, thinking there couldn't be a large enough number of guests, even at full capacity, for the lodge to make the money needed to run and maintain a small ski resort.

2

"Town residents can purchase lift tickets or passes, as can the guests from the other, larger resorts." Rocky motioned toward a rack full of brochures. "People staying in Aspen come out to Crow Creek for our events and often will get in a little bit of skiing while here. Our slopes are less crowded than those at the big resorts, and our trails have been written up in several magazines. We're gaining quite a reputation for cross country skiing."

It sounded lovely. It *all* sounded lovely. This was going to be an amazing trip. Honestly, I'd been excited since the judge had told me he'd included me in his family vacation plans, and I'd been on cloud nine since leaving early this morning.

"How difficult are the slopes?" It was something that had been worrying me since the judge had invited me to come along. I hadn't been skiing in decades, and even then, I hadn't been all that good. I didn't want to ruin everyone's vacation by ending up in the hospital.

"We've got one intermediate and one easy slope on either side of the terrain park," Rocky indicated with a wave of his hand, "then one harder slope along with two trails where the chair lift lets you off. The trails are suitable for either cross-country or downhill skiing. They aren't really that challenging, but the views are stunning. The Easy Stroll is our most popular trail."

"Easy Stroll?" That sounded right up my alley.

He grinned and nodded. "Just like the name. It's a long path that loops back and forth across the side of the mountain. It's a long, gentle downward slope. We're expanding it on the one side to make it even longer and add on a third trail geared specifically toward cross-country skiers, but that section won't be ready for another few weeks."

The Easy Stroll. I was definitely making a note of that.

"Are we ready?" Judge Beck turned to me, keycards in

hand. "They went ahead and sent our luggage up, so if you want to check out the gift shop first, we can do that."

"Let's get settled in our room first," I suggested. With the time difference, it was only late morning. We'd have plenty of time to explore and shop later.

The judge called to the kids, and we headed up the stairs. The lodge was partially built on a slope, so even though we were heading to the second floor, we'd have a door off the common room that led outside. From there, it would be an easy downhill to get to where the chair lift was.

A short walk down a wide hallway, and we'd found the door marked two-two-one. Judge Beck swiped his card, opened the door, and we walked in.

"Wow."

The word came softly from Henry's lips as he stepped away from the door and surveyed our suite. Madison was equally impressed, but far too much the teenage girl to show it. Instead she glanced around, gave the common room with its huge fireplace an approving nod, then turned to her father.

"Which is Kay's and my room?"

Judge Beck smiled. "You and Henry work out who gets which room. No fighting," he added as the pair took off.

I'll admit I was gawking at the room much like Henry. I'd been gawking since we landed. Everywhere I turned, I felt like I was in the middle of a Bob Ross painting. Stands of evergreens with blobs of snow weighing down their branches. Black jagged mountains with thick white swaths where the ski resorts had groomed their trails. Warm yellow lights in the valley, humanizing the beautifully harsh, towering nature. Snow was everywhere, like icing liberally applied to every rooftop and handrail. And it was cold—so cold I felt my nose hairs freeze with every inhalation.

"Think that's real?" Judge Beck pointed to the bear-skin rug on the floor.

"I doubt it." I knelt down, eyeing the huge teeth. "I'm pretty sure the deer head is real, though."

"I'm not sure how I feel about dead animals watching me while I'm on vacation." The judge took a stroll around the room, opening a curtain and revealing a gorgeous view of the slopes.

A firm knock sounded. Henry shouted that he'd get it and raced to beat Madison to the door. In the hallway was a middle-aged woman with a steeply asymmetrical bob of blonde hair and a clipboard in her hands. She wore a pair of dark wash jeans with a knife-pleat down the front and a crisp salmon-colored button-down shirt. A barcoded tag hung from a lanyard at her neck.

"Welcome to Foxdancer Lodge, I'm Cheryl," she announced as I was wondering if she'd actually ironed her jeans. "I've got your itinerary, including the times you're scheduled to be fitted for your rentals. Before you head over, make sure you stop and get your badges at the kiosk in the gift shop."

Madison and Henry hopped with excitement as Cheryl handed me a folder.

"You signed up for the all-inclusive package, so your badges will let you on not only our lift, but the lifts at the other two resorts in Aspen," Cheryl continued. "You can also use the badges to buy stuff in the restaurant, the snack bar, and in the gift shop."

"We pick up the badges in the lodge's gift shop?" I asked, just to clarify.

She nodded. "Just ask the employee working the register. He's the badge guy."

I grinned, amused that it sounded like a title. The Badge Guy.

"We need to hustle up," Judge Beck told the kids. "Put all your things away. If we hurry at the rental place, we'll have time to play on the slopes before dinner."

That got the kids moving. The judge followed Henry into the room, leaving me with Cheryl who was pulling some brochures from under a paper on her clipboard. "I'm not sure if Rocky told you about any of this, but Crow Creek has a Wednesday night bonfire down on the town square."

I took the brochures. "His name is really Rocky Forrest?"

She chuckled. "It's Richard Forrest, but don't let him know I told you that. He goes by Rocky."

My boss called himself "Gator" Pierson on his YouTube videos, so it wasn't exactly a shock to hear our host had come up with a more interesting moniker than Richard.

"There's free hot cocoa, and the shops offer ten percent off any purchases," Cheryl continued. "Thursdays there are arts and crafts—for adults as well as kids! And each week our very own Peabody Mann gives a talk at the library on local history. It's very interesting. Guests say it's one of their favorite activities. He has wonderful stories about the local mine, notable ranches of the last century, and the notorious naughty-house that was next door to the church in the late nineteenth century."

Cheryl giggled infectiously at the last, and I couldn't help but join in. I loved quirky local history. The kids might be able to snowboard for twelve hours, but I'd probably be worn out after half a day of skiing. It was nice to know there were other interesting activities I could occupy my time with.

Crow Creek *was* a cute place. It reminded me a lot of Locust Point in a way. "I'm surprised you all have managed to stay apart from Aspen," I told her.

Cheryl straightened her shoulders. "We're an incorporated town, and we pride ourselves on keeping our own history and culture. Aspen can be as big-city as they want.

We're the place people come to when they want that clean wholesome small-town experience, with friendly people who know your name."

Big city? Aspen had a population of under eight thousand, last time I'd checked. That was hardly what I'd call big city, but then again, Crow Creek was probably less than a third of that. It was a cute town. I had no doubt that Cheryl did know every one of our names and had memorized pertinent facts about each of us.

"Thank you." I waved the brochures. "We'll definitely take the kids to some of these to give them a break, and I'm looking forward to hearing Peabody Mann talk about the history of the town."

"If there's anything I can help you with, please give me a call," Cheryl told me, pointing out the phone number on our agenda.

I closed the door behind her, setting the brochures and papers on a side table.

"Quite the Julie McCoy." Judge Beck came back into the main room, a pair of sturdy hiking shoes in hand.

"I'm surprised you know who Julie McCoy is," I teased. "Aren't you a little young for that show?"

"No one is too young for the *Love Boat*." He stuck the hiking shoes in the closet with our heavy jackets, then turned to me. "I watched a lot of reruns growing up. My Mom was in charge of the television, and you watched what she wanted, or you didn't watch anything at all."

"Those were the days when there were all of five channels to choose from," I mused.

"And the broadcast actually ended at midnight," he added.

"Leaving only a test pattern and that horrible loud tone until six in the morning." I smiled, remembering how I'd wake up early some mornings, get my bowl of Cheerios, and sit on the couch, staring at that test pattern as I waited for the early programming.

"Broadcasting started and ended with a still photo of the flag and the national anthem." Judge Beck shook his head. "And cartoons were only on Saturdays."

"Ah, the eagerly anticipated *Scooby Doo*. And *Josie and the Pussycats*."

"Y'all are old," Madison drawled, coming into the main room with her iPad. "I'll bet you watched the original *Scooby Doo* and not the new ones."

"Those were the best. Nothing beats original *Scooby Doo*," I told her. "What cartoons did you watch when you were little?"

I wasn't sure what cartoons were popular now or had been popular a decade ago when Madison had been young.

"*Teen Titans*." She shrugged. "*Johnny Test*."

Henry snorted as he came out of his room. "Right. Mom said you watched *Peppa Pig* nonstop."

Madison threw a decorative pillow at her brother. "Well, at least I wasn't watching *Dinosaur Train*. That show sucked."

"All I can say is that the *Thundercats* of my childhood definitely did not suck," Judge Beck announced. "Now, hurry up and unpack so we can get our badges, then head over to be fitted for snowboards and skis."

Once we were all settled into our rooms, we went downstairs and made our way to see The Badge Guy.

The Badge Guy was a short, portly, middle-aged man who was also running the cash register in the gift shop. He ushered us to a kiosk next to a display rack full of Foxdancer Lodge logo-emblazoned postcards and pulled a stack of plastic cards from a lockbox.

"Now, don't lose these," he warned Madison and Henry. "There's a ten-dollar fee to replace them. This is what gets you on all the lifts as well as allows you to charge stuff to your room."

"Do I want Madison and Henry to be able to charge stuff to the room?" the judge asked me as he eyed the stuffed animals, mugs, and t-shirts.

"We're all going to be off on our own," I reminded him. "They'll want to be able to grab something to eat or drink without needing to carry around cash. Besides, it's not like you'd say no if they wanted a t-shirt."

"True." He glanced over to The Badge Guy. "Cheryl said that these get us on *all* the lifts, right? Not just the ones here at the lodge?"

"Yep. You paid for the all-inclusive package. The first time you go to a resort, you'll need to wait in the lift ticket line. They'll scan the badge, put a sticker on it, then off you go. Next time you can go straight to the lifts."

"That's really convenient," I commented.

He nodded. "That's the idea. The accountants work out the costs behind the scenes, so you don't have to. We've even started doing it for staff and instructors. Foxdancer Lodge employees get access to the other resort's amenities, even outside of work, and the same with the other resort's employees. Makes it feel like one giant resort instead of four or five."

He gestured for Madison to step up to the camera, took her picture, then printed out a badge. Before he handed it to her, he strung it on a red lanyard and again warned her not to lose it. The judge went next while Madison and I inspected the badge.

The picture must have been for verification in case she needed to replace it, because her badge had nothing on it besides a blue stripe, the lodge's logo, and a bar code with a number under it. There was a lot of white space along the sides, I supposed for the other resorts to put their stickers.

Judge Beck's card came back just like Madison's, only with a different number and without the blue stripe across the upper right corner.

"What's the stripe for?" I asked The Badge Guy.

"It means you're under twenty-one and can't drink." He shot Henry a grin. "And before you think about switching with your dad and ordering a beer, know that the pictures I'm taking go into a database and pull up on the screen when the badge is scanned."

"I don't like beer," Henry announced.

"I know you'd never try something like that," his father said. "But it's reassuring to know that if we lose our badge, someone isn't going to go hog wild on our account."

"The pictures help, but still report a missing badge right away," The Badge Guy reminded us. "We'll lock the number down and reissue a new one so that sort of thing doesn't happen."

"I take it you have to replace a lot of missing badges?" I asked as I stepped up to the camera.

"Mostly instructors and staff," he said. "They're wearing a badge every day, five days a week, all season, so there's more opportunity for one to fall out of a coat pocket or catch on something and come off." He held up my badge in one hand and the lanyard in another and pulled. They came apart with snap. "Safety feature. But safety means sometimes one pops off and the owner doesn't realize it until they go to grab a hot chocolate."

"Wouldn't the lift attendant notice it was missing?" I watched as he threaded my badge onto another lanyard.

"They should, but once they see you a few times in a day, they don't worry as much about looking at your badge every ride up the mountain." He handed me the plastic card. "People tuck them in their jackets so they don't flap around when they're flying down the slopes. They're supposed to pull them out and show them every time they take a lift up, but like I said, if the operator recognizes you, sometimes they don't bother to ask. My aunt works one of the lifts at Snowmass on weekends. They get busy. Plus, they don't want to annoy customers by pestering them over and over for their badge."

I believed that customers shouldn't be getting annoyed at employees doing their jobs, but I'd seen enough cashiers being yelled at over the years to completely sympathize.

My badge, just like the judge's, was minus a blue stripe across the corner. I quickly realized that figuring out whose badge was whose was going to be an issue. We'd most likely be tossing belongings all over the common area of our suite, and it was entirely likely that the adults and the kids might end up with the wrong badges.

"Can we put our initials on the back in Sharpie or something to keep them straight?" I asked The Badge Guy.

"You can, but we've come up with a better idea." He pulled out a tray full of stickers and set it on the counter. "Choose carefully because these have the same glue the resorts use on their stickers. Once you put them on, they're not coming off."

Choosing was definitely hard. They were all animal stickers, and there must have been twenty different kinds.

"Am I a trout or a mountain lion?" I asked as we all huddled over the tray.

"How about a moose?" Henry suggested. "Or this wolf? I like the wolf."

"You get the wolf," I told him. "I've changed my mind. I'm taking this bighorn sheep."

"Bison or bear. Bison or bear," Judge Beck mused.

"Bison," I told him. "Definitely bison."

"I can't decide between the hawk or the wild horse. Ooh! What's this? It looks like a prairie dog or something."

The Badge Guy leaned over the counter. "It's a pika.

They're like little rabbits with short round ears. You find them up in the mountains, usually in the boulder fields. That's the last pika sticker we've got. I'll have to remember to order more."

"It's adorable." Madison picked up the pika sticker, then bit her lip. "But the hawk…and the mustang."

The Badge Guy laughed. "Take all three. You won't be the first one with the back of your badge loaded in stickers."

She gave the man a bright smile, thanked him, then put the stickers in her coat pocket. "I'll decide which one to use later. Maybe I'll put the other two on my school notebooks."

"We sell whole sets of these stickers without the industrial strength glue." The Badge Guy gestured toward the front of the store and yet another display case.

Madison ended up buying a book of stickers, then a second book to give to a friend, while Henry picked up a t-shirt and a mug. We browsed for a while, then Judge Beck herded us out of the gift shop before we went crazy with the purchases.

"Come on. We need to get going or we'll be late for our rental fittings," he said.

Glancing at the lobby clock, I realized he was right. I followed them out into the parking lot, fingering my new badge and marveling at how technology had made the whole process so convenient.

One badge for everything. Linked to a database with my name, our room number, all of our personal information, and the judge's credit card. So much information on one little piece of plastic.

CHAPTER 2

$\mathcal{W}$e all climbed into the huge SUV that Judge Beck had rented and drove into Snowmass Village. Parking near the resort, we headed into a shop filled with everything from snowshoes to snowmobiles. The front section of the store was busy with shoppers buying clothing, equipment, and accessories, where the back end housed a huge rental area. Hanging outside the doorway to the rental shop were information sheets highlighting the various instructors, complete with a head shot, a brief bio, and what their specialty areas were. I saw Madison scanning them, her eyes snagging on the picture of a very handsome, young, blond man who was probably five to six years older than her.

We entered, signed in, then stood around and waited for our appointments. Judge Beck hovered near me, a worried expression on his face.

"Second thoughts?" I asked him. "Are you nervous about the kids getting hurt?"

"No. I mean, yes, but it's not like they haven't been skiing before. This is the first time they've snowboarded, but I made sure they had lessons with good instructors, and safety equipment. No, I just needed to ask—or tell—you something."

I tilted my head and regarded him, amused to see him so flustered. "Okay."

"I wasn't sure…I mean, you said it had been a long time since you'd skied." The judge ran a hand through his hair.

It had been, and I was more than a little concerned about what was going to happen the first time I snapped into my skis. But I hadn't expected the judge to be thinking about my athletic ability—or lack thereof.

"What do you want to ask—or tell—me?" I asked.

He took a deep breath. "I bought you a set of daily ski lessons, just like I bought snowboard lessons for the kids, but I'm thinking I shouldn't have. I don't want you to feel insulted, like I think you can't ski. If you don't want the lessons, that's fine. I can cancel them."

It was comforting to know that a paid instructor would have a chance to give me a few tune-up lessons before the judge or the kids witnessed my attempts at tackling more than the bunny slopes. Hopefully, this instructor was good enough that by the time I joined the others, I'd actually look like I knew what I was doing.

"I would love ski lessons." I waited for his relieved smile. "Thank you. That was very thoughtful of you, and I appreciate it. It *has* been a long time since I skied, and I've only been on the slopes out east. Even then, I was never the most confident skier. Lessons will really help me enjoy our vacation more."

His expression warmed. "Good. And do you want to ski with me tonight at the lodge? I thought after dinner we all could play around on some of the slopes at our resort, then hit one of the bigger places tomorrow."

I thought of the trail that Rocky had mentioned and

nodded. "I'd love that but take it slow. No showing off and making me feel like a total klutz."

He held up a hand. "I promise."

"There's a long easy downhill trail that the owner mentioned when we were checking in," I told him. "It's called the Easy Stroll."

He nodded. "That sounds great. The kids will be on the terrain park all night, so we can take our time."

A trial run on the Easy Stroll was a good idea. It would help me get used to being on skis again after so long. "It's a date. But no laughing at me."

They called our names before he could reply, and we all split up. Henry and Madison went off to get snowboards while Judge Beck and I were fitted for skis. A young man not much older than Madison led me off to the side, introducing himself as Red. Nothing about Red was Red except for his crimson t-shirt. He had golden-brown skin, dark eyes, and wild tight curls that had been bleached at the tips and dyed gold. Red was tall and wiry with a smooth agile grace that was as charming as his smile.

"What's your skiing experience, Ms. Carrera?" he asked as he measured my feet for boots.

"In my twenties, I was on the slopes three or four times each winter," I told him. "I got reasonably comfortable on the intermediate trails, but that was it. And that was a long time ago. I'm probably going to stay on the beginner slopes this week."

"You'll be on black diamonds before you know it," he said cheerfully.

I shuddered. "Not then and not now. The black diamond slopes always scared me."

He smiled up at me, and I noted his adorable dimples. "Too steep?"

"That and the moguls. I could never figure out how to get

15

through a mogul field without winding up on my back with my skis flying on their own down the slope."

He laughed. "You've got the package with lessons. I don't know who your instructor will be but ask them to help you with that. I'm assuming most of your experience is east coast skiing?"

"All of it."

He grimaced. "That's more like ice skating than skiing. There's never enough powder out east."

My mind went back to the scrape sound my edges would make as I turned on the slopes, how the trails were smooth and hard, with some "corn" and, if we were lucky, a light pile of powder pushed all the way to the sides. I was eager, and more than a little apprehensive, to experience the slopes here, but it had ages since I'd done this.

"The last time I skied was probably thirty years ago. I'm not sure I even remember how," I confessed. Was it truly like riding a bike?

"You'll be fine. Book a few extra private instruction sessions if you're worried about getting back up to speed." Red stood and glanced over at where the gorgeous blond man from the instructor bios was fitting Madison. She was smiling up at the young Adonis and digging something out of her pocket. Pulling his badge toward her, she ran her fingers over the plastic, then let it drop back to his chest. Madison laughed at something the blond man said, and I saw an expression settle on Red's face, as if he'd been struck by a lightning bolt.

Aww. Young love. Or attraction, at the very least.

"Are you also an instructor, Red?" I asked. "A snow-boarding instructor, perhaps?"

"Yeah." He shook his head, forcing his gaze away from Madison. "She's your daughter?"

"My friend's daughter. She's skied before, but this will be her first time snowboarding."

A slow grin spread across his face. "Yeah?"

"Yeah."

"Then I might need to take a look at the instructor schedule." He turned away and went over to bunch of skis, pulling a pair off the rack. "I'm going to start you off with these. They're not super stable at high speeds, but they're easily maneuverable. Once you get the hang of it and are ready to hit the more challenging slopes, come back in and I'll get you a longer pair."

Red went into the back room to adjust the bindings and get me a pair of boots. Madison walked over to me in her stocking feet, shooting a quick glance at the blond who'd been helping her.

"His name's Luke."

I lifted my eyebrows at the dreamy tone of her voice. Luke had to be early twenties—too old for a girl still in high school.

"Your father would have a fit," I told her. I'd been sixteen once. At her age, it wouldn't be unusual for her to flirt with the young, good-looking instructors, but I also hoped Madison didn't let the excitement of a vacation carry her away. She was a smart, thoughtful girl, but even so, I was pretty sure Judge Beck would be watching her like a hawk the whole week.

Madison headed back to where she'd been sitting, sending me a saucy grin over her shoulder. "Think he'll be my instructor for the week?"

I trusted Madison, but I didn't know this Luke at all. While Madison wasn't likely to throw sense out the window for some boy, this young man was *very* good looking. Maybe I should have a word with Luke, pointing out to him that Madison was only sixteen. And that her father was a judge.

Surely he'd know. It was on her profile. Her badge had a blue stripe across the corner that indicated she was under twenty-one and wouldn't be able to buy alcoholic beverages. He *had* to know she was too young. Far too young.

"Ms. Carrera?"

I turned to see Red holding out a pair of boots for me to try on. I shoved my feet in the boots, feeling like I was about to take one giant leap for mankind onto the moon surface as I stood up.

"Well, these things certainly haven't changed in the last thirty years," I joked.

"The skis sure have." He pointed to the pair he'd pulled out for me.

Before I knew it, we were all loading our gear into the SUV and looking at our schedules for instructors for tomorrow morning.

Madison squealed. "Luke is teaching me tomorrow! Luke Shipley," she read off the sheet.

"I've got Skittles Hackset," Henry announced. "I'm thinking anyone named Skittles is probably an expert snowboarder and not just some pretty blond boy trying to pick up snow-bunnies on the slopes."

Madison punched her brother in the shoulder. "Luke is an expert snowboarder. See? It says right here on his bio."

"Gus Johnson is my instructor," I told them. "Supposedly he excels in making sure old lady skiers don't break a hip trying to keep up with their young friends."

"It does not say that." Madison laughed and leaned over my shoulder. "Oh, cool. He subbed on the Olympic ski jumping team back in the nineties."

"Before you were born," the judge told her. "He's probably around my age."

We loaded into the SUV and chatted on the return trip to

the lodge. Back in the room, I stacked my gear in the living area while the kids raced out, eager to try the slopes behind our suite.

"What are you up for?" Judge Beck poked his head out of the room he and Henry were sharing. "Do you want to do the Easy Stroll now or after dinner?"

"After dinner." Hopefully by then I would have worked up enough nerve.

"That leaves a few hours. Do you want to join the kids? Go shopping? Do those arts and crafts that Cheryl woman was talking about?"

"That's on Thursday," I reminded him. "I might go downstairs, check out the menu and the events board. Then I'm thinking that I'll take a snack and a book outside and watch the kids go down the slopes."

The judge moved fully into the common room. "I've got some work I need to deal with, but maybe I'll join you later."

"Work?" I shook a finger at him. "We're on vacation."

His eyebrows shot up. "So, I didn't see you checking your e-mails at least three times since we left home?"

He'd noticed? "Molly just started, and she's not trained in anything but basic skip tracing. You know how J.T. is. In and out of the office. She's in over her head."

"And I'll be returning to a full docket. I've got more initial pleadings than I've got fingers."

"I'll make you a deal. I'll buy us lunch and meet you on the back patio in half an hour."

He turned to look back in his bedroom. "I really can't."

Oh, for Pete's sake. Some of my best memories were of us working late into the night at the dining room table, but this was a vacation. I understood the need to juggle work, family, and play, but I hated that he was spending the entire afternoon of our first day here with his nose in a bunch of papers.

He must have seen my disappointed expression because he took a few steps toward me. "If I can knock all this out right now, then I won't have it hanging over me the rest of the week."

I eyed him. "So, you're saying just this one afternoon and you won't be checking e-mails or making calls for the rest of the week?"

He sighed and ran a hand through his hair. "I can't promise that. But hopefully I won't need to do more than check and make a quick response. I wanted to get all this done before we left, but I couldn't manage it. I'm sorry. I know we're supposed to be on vacation. I want to spend time with you and the kids. I won't make this a regular thing."

There was a slight defensiveness to his voice, as if he'd had this discussion a lot—probably with Heather. I didn't want to have his work be an area of friction between us, and honestly it wasn't. I worked hard as well. I admired that in him just as I'd admired that trait in Eli. But I knew how he regretted not being around much when his kids were young, and I didn't want him to look back on this time with regret as well.

"You'll be done by dinner?" I asked instead.

"I'll be done by dinner," he promised. "And after dinner, you and I can ski the Easy Stroll."

My stomach twisted at the reminder, and I found myself hoping that the path was as easy and stroll-like as our host had claimed. "Deal."

* * *

I SCARFED down some cheese and crackers, read, and watched the kids spend more time on their butts than on their snowboards. By the time we'd cleaned up and headed down at four for an early dinner, I was completely relaxed and in vacation-mode. The dining room was packed, and the lodge staff were making the rounds, greeting each guest and spending a few moments ensuring they were enjoying their stay. We'd just finished our salads when Rocky Forrest stopped by our table.

Rocky still had on the dark-wash jeans but had swapped out his green cowboy shirt for a royal blue lodge-logo one. Lines creased the dark tanned skin at the corner of his eyes and bracketed his smiling mouth. I looked at him, thinking that he struck me as the sort of guy who ate organic, shopped at farmer's markets, and took care to ensure everything he bought was fair trade. I was willing to bet that back in his college days, he'd smelled like patchouli.

"Are you all ready to hit the slopes!" He clapped his hands enthusiastically then rubbed them together.

"I'm going back out to the terrain park right after dinner," Henry announced. "How late is it open?"

"We keep the lights on and the rope and J-bar lifts going on the park and the slopes until ten. If the rest of you are wanting to do the trails, the chair lift runs until six, but any of us at the desk are happy to send you up any time after. During a full moon, the Puma Trail is bright as day. You don't even need the lights."

"I'm hoping there are no actual pumas on the Puma Trail," I teased.

Rocky held up both hands. "Oh, no, ma'am. It's perfectly safe. Everything in Crow Creek is safe. No animal attacks. No people attacks. No crime at all to speak of. People don't even jaywalk here."

"I'll be extra careful to use marked crosswalks when I'm shopping downtown," I assured him. His portrayal of squeaky-clean Crow Creek was amusing. I lived in a little town, and I knew how locals kept their secrets. Every town had crime; small towns were just better at hiding it than the cities, in my experience.

"Deputy Raine would just give you a warning." He shook his finger at me, his grin revealing straight white teeth. "It's bad business to go around ticketing tourists."

"Especially over jaywalking," Judge Beck drawled.

"Stop by the front desk for trail maps before you all head out tonight. And don't forget the lecture series at the library this week." Rocky patted Henry on the shoulder. His phone rang and he pulled it from his pocket, headed back out into the lobby as he answered.

"Is he for real?" Madison rolled her eyes. "All that cheer and goodwill? He's like a skinny Santa Claus."

"It would be difficult to manage a ski lodge if you were grumpy," her father countered. "It's part of his job to make sure the guests are happy and that we want to come back. And clearly it works. Stuart and Karen come here every year and recommended it. The place is packed. I was lucky to get us the suite. They're usually sold out a year ahead of time."

"I think he's nice," Henry announced. "I was talking to him when we were checking in, and he told me his family has been in Crow Creek for six generations. He's a member of the historic trust and the town tourism board. He really wants Crow Creek to be the same clean, happy small town it was when he was a kid."

"Cheryl's on the town tourism board too," Madison pointed out. "I read it on some award plaque up by the front desk."

The locals seemed to be a tight-knit group who valued their history and their town. I didn't blame them. Eli and I had moved to Locust Point when we'd first gotten married, attracted to the same sort of things these people wanted to preserve in Crow Creek. But now I saw proposed zoning changes, developments where farmland had once stood. The larger city of Milford had been annexing areas and spreading closer and closer to our town limits. I hated thinking about it, but it seemed just a matter of time until Locust Point was nothing but a suburb glued to the edge of a larger city.

I hoped that didn't happen to Crow Creek.

"I might want to check out the downtown area later this week," Henry commented. "Maybe after I've been snow-boarding a few days and need a break."

"I'd like to eventually go downtown and do some shopping as well," I told him. "You can come with me, or if you don't want to leave the terrain park, I can always look for whatever you need."

Maybe I could convince him to join me for that speaker at the library. Henry loved history. I had no doubt that he would enjoy hearing about the old mining camps, ranches, and that turn-of-the-century house of prostitution next to the church, but he was still a teenage boy, and the lure of the snowboard was strong right now.

After dinner, we went our separate ways. The kids headed to the terrain park. Judge Beck offered to run upstairs, grab our equipment, and meet me in the lobby.

While I waited for him, I popped into the gift shop. I really wanted to go downtown to pick up a few things for my friends, but ended up grabbing a picture-holder/refrigerator magnet that had the lodge logo complete with the dancing fox on it. I needed to make sure I got a shot of the four of us with our gear before we left, then this picture could go on the fridge next to the one Eli had taken of me at the beach.

New memories. Another new part of my life. There had been my childhood, then that brief slice of single adulthood, then my long rich life with Eli. Who knew what the future would bring, but for now, I had friends and a rewarding job. I was surrounded by people I loved, and I was enjoying every minute of it. I put the magnet and the book on the counter and dug for my wallet in my purse, thinking how amazing life still was, how many amazing things were coming my way each and every day.

CHAPTER 3

I eyed the lift with some anxiety. "Getting on these things always reminded me of trying to time when I should hop in on a game of double-dutch in jump rope."

Judge Beck shook his head. "Double-what? I have no idea what that is."

I waved a hand at the speeding chairs, whipping around the corner to collect a pair of skiers. "It's like jump rope. You've got seconds between when the chair scoops up the people in front of you and when the next chair is *right there* for you. That's seconds to hurriedly scoot yourself with these long skis across a narrow, flat area, get yourself in position, and basically brace for impact before the chair smacks you in the back of your thighs."

The judge shot me a worried glance. "What are you saying? Should I ask the lift operator to slow the chairs? Get ready to grab you and yank you into place? Watch out in case you smack me in the face with a ski pole?"

I forced my expression to remain solemn. "Did I ever tell you about the time I knocked my boyfriend off the lift?"

He sucked in a breath. "I'll make sure we pull the bar

down when we're on. We should anyway, you know. It's always best to be safe."

"It was at the end of the lift when we were getting off," I explained. "Just like getting on, I panic a little about the timing, because if you don't get off, then you end up going around the corner on the lift, and they have to stop the whole thing, then try to get you off. It's very embarrassing."

Judge Beck eyed me. Horrified. Speechless.

"And then if you *do* manage to get off the lift, you have to time it so the chair gently pushes you forward and away, otherwise the chair knocks you over and they have to stop the lift and drag you out of the way."

"Uhhh."

That was all the judge managed to say. I kept a straight face as we edged forward.

"Anyway, I was riding the lift with Doug. We were both freshmen in college and had gone skiing this one weekend. I went to get off the lift, and in my hurry, I accidently elbowed him and knocked him over. That's how I know they have to stop the lift and drag you out of the way when you fall."

Judge Beck's lips twitched. "I take it that was the end of your relationship with Doug."

"Yes. Yes, it was." We edged forward a few more steps. "It might be wise for you to take a different chair than me. Just in case."

"I'll take my chances." The judge grinned. "Kay, you're pulling my leg, right? None of this *really* happened, right?"

I laughed. "Actually, it did, but I did stretch the truth a bit. Doug managed to get away from the chair lift, but he *did* wipe out about ten feet past where we unloaded. And it *was* my fault."

"Noted. Keep an eye on Kay's elbows when getting off the lift. How about getting on? Shall I expect you to knock me into the operator while we're trying to get on?"

"No. Maybe. I'm not sure. It has been a long time since I've skied, and I do tend to get anxious about lifts."

"I should have had that brandy after dinner," Judge Beck muttered as we skied up to the lift.

We got on without incident, lowering the bar right after we were seated and resting our skis on the metal support as we ascended. I craned my neck to look over at the terrain park, the fading daylight casting long shadows over the snow. A faint shriek and a laugh rent the air, and I saw a girl with long dark hair under her helmet spin around on her snowboard, fall to her rear, and slide about ten feet down the slope. As she came to a rest, a boy with a black-and-neon-blue jacket slid past her on his butt, trying to slow himself enough to get back on his feet.

"Good thing I bought them a week's worth of private lessons," Judge Beck muttered. "They're terrible."

I laughed. "It's the first time they've ever been on snowboards. *I've* been skiing before, and there's still a strong chance I'm going to knock you off the lift."

"Then it's a good thing I bought you a week's worth of lessons as well." The judge laughed. "Kay, I'm worried. Are you really that bad? Am I going to need to try to find a cell signal and get the ski patrol to come haul you off the mountain? Or haul *me* off on a stretcher because you've elbowed me into a tree?"

It was a possibility. "Okay, I'm sort of kidding. Outside of the incident with poor Doug—which in my defense, I *was* very nervous since it was our first date—I haven't had anything horrible happen. But it has been a long time since I've skied, and I'm worried that it's not exactly like the old riding-a-bicycle adage. And to be honest, I wasn't all that great of a skier even back when I *was* going regularly."

"Once you're heading down the slope, it will all come back to you," he assured me. "You'll be fine."

I hoped so, because what I wasn't telling him was that I was just as nervous as on that first date with Doug. I didn't want the judge to see me sprawled on my backside or plowing face-first into a tree, or having to hobble down the slope knee-deep in snow because I fell and one of my skis came off and shot down the hill ahead of me.

I needed to do something to take my mind off the very likely possibility I was going to make a total fool of myself in front of the judge. So, I changed the subject.

"Did you notice how Madison was all aflutter over the blond boy fitting her for her snowboard rental?" I eyed him knowingly. "I'm hoping you brought your shotgun with you."

Judge Beck laughed. "No, I didn't bring a shotgun, and yes, I did see that. I made sure the young man in question knows that she is sixteen, and management has assured me that she will be absolutely safe in his—or any of the other instructors'—presence."

I looked over at him. "So you're not worried?"

He sighed. "I'm always worried, but I'm stepping back and having faith in both my daughter and the staff. Me jumping in, lecturing her and changing the schedule so her instructor is an eighty-year old eunuch isn't going to do anything but ruin our vacation and teach Madison that I don't trust her."

I bit back a smile because I heard the frustration in his voice. "You're a good father."

There was a moment of silence before his response. "Yeah. I am. And I probably should have brought a shotgun."

I laughed. "On the other hand, I quite liked the young man who fitted me for my skis. Red. Very charming, polite boy, and quite knowledgeable."

He turned to look at me. "Red, huh? Should I be jealous?"

Jealous? *Jealous?* The very thought that Judge Beck would even joke about being jealous of another man's attentions to me had my mind spinning. At that moment, I was very glad we'd lowered the safety bar, or there was a good chance I might have fallen off the lift and taken him with me.

I struggled to gain control of my thoughts and emotions. He was kidding. We were friends. Yes, there might be something, some possibility, hovering around the end of our friendship, but I wasn't about to read anything into his joking statement. Because he was definitely joking.

I snorted. "Red? He's young enough to be my grandson. I meant he might be a better instructor for Madison than Luke. At least he's under twenty-one from the blue stripe on his badge. I'm betting he's either a senior in high school or newly graduated."

Judge Beck lifted his hands. "I'm going to leave this all up to fate. You can play the matchmaker with my daughter. I'm too invested to see potential beaus as anything other than a danger, so I'm bowing out. Madison is smart, and outside of that one time she snuck out last spring, she's always proven herself to be worthy of mine and Heather's trust. If she wants to have a harmless flirtation this vacation, I'm not going to worry—whether it's with Luke, or Red, or an eighty-year old eunuch."

"Eww." I laughed. "Now, how about Henry? Was he eyeing any of the instructors? Do we see a winter vacation romance in the near future for our young man?"

"Henry is all about the snowboard right now. Besides, there's only one romance I'm worried about this week," Judge Beck added with a mutter. Before I could even wonder at his meaning, we were raising the safety bar and preparing to dismount from the lift. Thankfully, the judge remained out of elbow-reach and wisely moved ahead of me as we exited the chair. I instinctively balanced on my skis and zipped down the slight hill to the flat section where the various trails and slopes all converged, thinking that maybe the judge was right. I shifted my skis sideways to stop and slid around—then kept going in a three-sixty that wound up with me on my rear, skis crossed in the back and pointed to opposite directions in the front.

The judge spun around on his skis, gracefully sliding a few feet backward before stopping with seemingly no effort at all. "Kay!"

"I'm fine." It took me a few tries to get up. "Just got a little enthusiastic trying to stop."

He skated forward, his brow furrowed. "If you decide you don't feel like skiing, there are other things for us to do tonight."

Little late for that given that we were on the top of a mountain with only one way down.

"I just want you to have fun on this vacation," he added.

I'd been so worried that I'd make a fool of myself in front of them—in front of *him*. Suddenly all that fell away. He just wanted me to have fun. And if that meant I was watching them ski while sipping hot toddies and reading a book, it wouldn't bother him. I was still anxious about the lift, the black diamonds, and the moguls, but at this moment I was a whole lot less anxious about him seeing me slide down the mountain on my rear.

"I like skiing. I've always liked skiing." I elbowed him—gently, because even though we weren't on the lift, I didn't want to inadvertently knock him over. "You don't have to be good at something to enjoy doing it. I was a mediocre skier in my twenties, and even with a week of instruction, I'll probably still be a mediocre skier. That has no bearing on whether I'm having fun or not. Henry might want to rule the terrain park by the time he leaves Colorado, but I've got different goals."

He tiled his head as he regarded me. "Which are?"

Far too complicated to confess right now. "I want to see beautiful scenery. I want to watch the kids laugh and play. To experience new things this week. To feel a sense of wonder and awe at least once a day."

"Well, are you ready to experience the wonder and awe of the Easy Stroll?" He smiled tentatively.

Was I? I looked at the slopes that headed down the mountain, flanking the terrain park at the bottom as they led straight toward the lodge. It was probably a steeper heading down that way than any trail named Easy Stoll could possibly be. Three teens shouted as they took off down the left slope. Two women shot past us to a steep intermediate slope marked with a blue square. The easiest way down was probably the trail we'd originally intended on taking. It might be dark by the time we made it to our suite, but I was here to have fun. I was here to experience wonder and awe. And I wasn't going to let some silly fears steal that from me.

"Yes, I'm ready."

The judge smiled and the pair of us shuffled along the ridge to a narrow winding path that gently led down into the woods.

"You first." Judge Beck waved me ahead. I pushed forward, hoping I didn't further embarrass myself.

My nervousness eased within the first fifteen minutes. The narrowness of the trail meant there wasn't much room to traverse the slope and slow down, but thankfully the path wasn't steep. The thick powder slowed my descent and gave me a lot more control than I'd ever had on the east coast slopes. We eased back and forth around the side of the mountain where I glimpsed the long bare patches of white of the other slopes, as well as the dark blots of the lodge and cabins. I paused to catch my breath and appreciate the scenery, then we headed down another path that should take us in a loop, eventually joining a wider slope leading down to the lodge.

As I skied, I quickly grew accustomed to the speed and

the weight of the boots and skis, and I relaxed. Judge Beck moved up to my side once he realized he wasn't going to need to scrape me up off the snow every few feet, then moved slightly ahead once the trail narrowed further. A few times we stopped to rest and admire the thick groves of pines and the occasional herd of deer off in the distance. The trail branched off a few times, and I noted that the judge always took the choice that seemed less steep.

This was…wonderful. Outside of that minor fall at the top of the mountain, I'd managed to stay on my feet, and with each push of my skis, the movement felt more and more natural. I might not be ready for those black diamond slopes or moguls, but at least I felt confident that I'd not make a complete fool out of myself this vacation.

We made one turn, then another. After a while, I started to worry. We should have seen the lodge by now or at least another skier. Plus, the path we were on was becoming increasingly narrow and flat. Relief flooded through me when the path widened out enough for me to pass the judge, but then I started to worry again when I realized the snow we were on wasn't as groomed as the trail had originally been.

I slowed to a stop and Judge Beck pulled up beside me, spraying snow in a move that was one hundred percent show-off.

"I don't think this is part of the trail. Did we make a wrong turn?" I asked.

The judge slid his goggles up on his forehead, pushing silver-streaked blond hair upward into a spiked row. "It's a little rugged. Didn't the manager say cross-country skiers use these trails? Maybe they're supposed to be rough."

This did not feel like it was part of the lodge trail system, but then again, I'd never skied out west before. "Let's check the map," I suggested. "Rocky said there was a side trail that wasn't open yet. I wonder if we somehow accidently got on it."

Judge Beck looked at me as if I'd lost my mind. "I don't have a map."

I rolled my eyes, thinking that this was something Eli would have done. Then I pulled off a glove and dug into a pocket for *my* map.

"Don't tell me. You never pull over and ask for directions when you're lost either," I teased as I unfolded the map.

He grinned. "I'm *never* lost. And if I were, I'd just use my special guy-GPS, and I'd be right back on track."

Holding the map in both hands, I tried to trace the trail we'd skied. "Were we supposed to take that right through the woods? On the map, it looks like the turn is farther down."

Judge Beck went to look over my shoulder, and I yanked the map away. "What happened to your special guy-GPS?" I teased.

He snatched the map out of my hands. "I can't even get a cell signal up here. How do you expect me to access my special guy-GPS skills?"

I chuckled, then watched him try to hide his dismay as he read the map.

"We're lost, aren't we?" I asked, wondering how many miles we were going to need to hike in boots, carrying our skis and poles. "Is there a flare or something we can send up?"

He sighed and glanced behind him. "We could trek back up this trail to where we made the wrong turn."

I winced, because that would be a long hike. I wasn't sure I could manage climbing back up, especially carrying skis. Looking down the hill a bit, I noticed that an unpaved road was within view and only about a quarter mile away, but the red truck currently driving on it was probably the only vehicle that had traveled the road in the last few hours—and it was too far away for us to hail.

"Maybe we should head down to that road and call the lodge?" the judge suggested. "I'm sure to get some kind of cell signal down there. Or we can keep going along this trail. It eventually circles back around to the lodge, but it looks like most of it is pretty flat."

Which meant we'd be powering ourselves along even ground in downhill skis. Plus, it was quickly growing dark and all we had for light was our cell phones.

"Or we can keep going, then make a left," I suggested, pointing to the map. "There's a farm or something right over here. They've got to have a phone or maybe they can give us a lift back to the lodge."

He looked at the map, then off in the direction of the farm. A faint curl of smoke teased up through the tree line, giving me hope that the residents were home with their woodstove warming their house.

Something about the expression on the judge's face tugged at my heart. He was blaming himself for this, even though it wasn't his fault we'd taken the wrong turn. I'd learned that's how he was. He took responsibility for everything. The buck always stopped with him, and he was always felt it was his duty to clean up the mess and make things right. I liked that about him, but it made me sad that he shouldered burdens he would have been justified in leaving by the side of the road.

I snatched the map away from him and shoved it back into my pocket. "I ask to experience wonder and adventure in this vacation, and I got it. We're bushwhacking through the mountains on skis, on a trail that isn't supposed to be open for another few weeks. There's a not-so-obvious fork in the rustic trail, and a decision needs to be made."

His lips twitched. "And which choice will we make, intrepid explorers that we are?"

"To go on, of course! I'll bet there's a nice family in that farmhouse who will give us hot chocolate and tell us wild stories of Colorado cattle drives while we warm up. Then they'll loan us their truck, or snowmobiles, to get back to the lodge, saying they'll pick them up later."

He snorted. "Or they'll shoot at us, telling us to get off their property."

"That's an adventure, too." I put my gloves back on.

The judge dug in his pocket and pulled out his cell phone, checking the signal. "Let's do it. Even if no one's home, I should be able to get a cell signal out in the open."

"Sounds like a plan to me. Beat you to the farmhouse? Loser brings a bottle of champagne to the hot tub tomorrow night?"

He looked at me, something soft and warm in his hazel eyes. Then he shoved his cell phone back in his pocket. "You're on."

Judge Beck reached the bottom of the mountain first, which wasn't exactly a surprise. He could have totally dusted me, but from the way he kept glancing back, I could tell he was slowing himself, just in case I fell and needed help.

We had to ski through a field and a stand of pines to get to the farm. I was so busy watching where I put my feet that I didn't even notice the faint curl of smoke we'd seen earlier had turned into a billowing black mass rising in the air.

Looking up as we came out into the open, I saw an old farmhouse with several outbuildings and a dark-colored SUV parked out front. The smoke was coming from a large bank barn. I couldn't see any actual flames, but that much smoke couldn't be good.

I stopped beside the judge, staring at what surely was a

fire, wondering if anyone had called it in. Was anyone home? Were the neighbors too far away to notice?

Before I could ask, the judge had his gloves off and his phone out. Grumbling about having only one bar, he punched in 911. There was some difficulty in telling the operator where the emergency was since we were lost. Neither of us knew the names of the nearest roads or even an address. Judge Beck ended up describing the farm and telling the operator how we'd managed to get here from the trail.

"They're sending a truck out," he told me when he'd hung up. "The woman said she was pretty sure we're at the old Shipley farm. Evidently the owner lives in Florida and leases it out."

I eyed the SUV and made a decision. "I don't see anyone. There might not be anyone home, but just in case, we should check."

We made our way toward the buildings as quickly as we could, taking off our skis and setting them safely aside near the SUV. The smoke was thick and acrid, flames now starting to show through cracks in the barn's siding. The judge clomped up to the front door of the house and pounded on it, calling out. I tried to look through the front windows, but there were thick black-out curtains or sheets over the glass. I eyed the snow for tracks. Some led from the front of the house toward the driveway where a set of tire tracks indicated there had been another vehicle here besides the SUV. Several sets of footsteps led to the barn and around the house. I wasn't sure when it had snowed last, but certainly if someone had been home, they would have come out to either greet us or to attempt to battle the fire in their barn.

"I don't think they're home," I called out to the judge before jogging around to the back of the house with my bulky boots, just to check. There were a few sets of footsteps there as well leading to stables behind the barn where the snow had been trampled and packed down. The stables weren't close enough to the barn to be on fire yet. I clomped back around front, hoping the fire department got here soon enough to save the other outbuildings and the house.

We grabbed our skis and moved a safe distance away, watching the barn burn for a few minutes before we heard the sound of sirens coming up the road. A pumper/tanker engine and a ladder truck arrived first, quickly followed by several sheriffs' cars and other rescue vehicles. While fire-fighters worked on the blaze, others ran long hoses out to a pond, chopping through the ice to get to the water. Judge Beck called the lodge, then called and left a message for both Madison and Henry that we would be late and that we'd meet them in our suite as soon as we returned. Then he started typing something on his phone.

"What are you doing?" If it had been Madison or Henry, I would have suspected they were posting a Snapchat update, but Judge Beck had never been active on social media.

"Uber. The woman at the front desk said the lodge van isn't available right now."

"Uber?" I laughed. "You're joking."

"It's that or catch a ride back with the fire department."

I looked over at the fire, realizing these guys would be busy for hours. I hadn't even thought about using an app to get a ride. "Do they come out this far?"

"Looks like they do." Judge Beck turned the phone toward me. It showed that a woman named Evie would be here in twenty minutes. The judge had noted in the comments that we were at the site of a working fire and to let us know when she arrived since we probably wouldn't see or hear the car with all the chaos. I nodded, admiring the judge's thorough-ness. He might not carry a map of the slopes, might not have

37

recognized we'd made a wrong turn, but he was certainly good at organizing a rescue.

As we watched the firefighters, a sheriff's deputy walked up to where we stood, pulling a battered notepad and pen out of his pocket. I recognized what was about to happen.

"I'm Deputy Raine. You the ones that called it in?" He looked us up and down, his gaze snagging on our skis propped up against the fence post. "Bit off the trails, aren't you?"

"We took a wrong turn and didn't realize it for a while," Judge Beck told him. "From the map, it looked like it would be easier to ski down here and call for someone to pick us up then hike back up the trail to the slope."

Deputy Raine nodded. "Glad you didn't get shot. This guy isn't too happy about trespassers."

Shot? So much for Rocky's version of friendly, crime-free Crow Creek. "He shoots people? We're not that far off the new trail, even though Rocky told us it wasn't due to be open for a few weeks."

The deputy snorted. "Rocky's being a bit optimistic, but that's nothing new. So, you all saw the fire from the trail and came to check it out?"

"We came to ask for a lift, and that's when we saw the fire," the judge explained. "It must have started fairly recently because from the trail it just looked like smoke from a wood-burning furnace."

Deputy Raine nodded. "Well, it's a good thing you were here. The closest neighbor is Cheryl Fisher, and she was at work when the call came in." He licked the end of his pencil and poised it above the notepad. "I'll need to know your names and where you're staying for the report, although I'm assuming you're at the lodge."

"Judge Nathaniel Beck and Kay Carrera," I told him. "And yes, we are staying at Foxdancer Lodge."

He grunted in approval. "It's small and cozy, but close to all the resorts. Cheryl works there." He pointed the pen toward the firefighters.

"Wait, *Cheryl* is a volunteer firefighter?" The pin-neat woman with a stack of brochures didn't fit with that image, but I should know better than to stereotype people.

The deputy nodded. "And hers is the place right down the road there. Neighbors, although the guy living here hasn't been around long. Cheryl's been in Crow Creek since she was a toddler."

Raine went back to his notepad. Judge Beck gave him our address back in Locust Point as well as our phone numbers and how long we were staying. The firefighters had a good stream of water coming from the pond now and were making headway on the fire. I glanced again over at the darkened house, noting the weathered wood siding and bleached roofing shingles.

"When did the people living here move in?" I asked, curious about how the fire had started. There were no livestock around, and the place looked unoccupied, even though there was a vehicle out front. The deputy had said the man hadn't lived here long, so that might account for the vacant feel of the place. The fire could have started with some faulty electrical wiring. Given the ramshackle state of the house, it seemed a possibility.

The deputy frowned. "A few months? The owner rents it out. It was vacant for years."

"The old Shipley Farm," I mused. "The owner lives in Florida."

Deputy Raine turned to me in surprise. "You know them? Or the Shipleys?"

Judge Beck shook his head. "No. The 911 operator told us the name and that the owner lived down in Florida. She said they lease the place out."

Deputy Raine rolled his eyes. "Maybelle is the worst gossip. It's probably why she took the job as our 911 operator."

"Do the Shipleys still own the farm?" I asked, feeling an immediate kinship to this Maybelle.

The deputy was quiet for a moment, watching the fire. "Nah. The owner bought the place at a tax sale about two years ago. Not sure what the heck he wanted with it, since he never lived here. Guess it was an investment rental for him, although from what I can tell, it was a piss-poor investment. It stood empty until this guy moved in. It used to be a nice farm. Darned shame to see it pass out of the family and slowly fall apart like this."

I eyed the enflamed barn and thought that this evening's events had dramatically speeded up the "falling apart."

"Do you think it might have been arson for the insurance money?" Judge Beck mused. "I've seen enough of that come through my courtroom over the years."

Deputy Raine shrugged. "Might be. The fire marshal will have to weigh in on that one."

I stood beside the two men, mirroring their stance as we all gazed at the fire.

"Seems like an odd place to rent out," I said. "The house looks like there hasn't been regular maintenance done in years, so I can't see it as having any appeal as a vacation rental—especially with all the lodges and inns in the area. And clearly whoever was leasing it wasn't using it as a working farm."

"People do rent houses for other reasons." Judge Beck shrugged. "Maybe it's inexpensive and suitable for someone who's working in town or at a nearby factory or something."

Were there factories in or around Aspen? I'd come here as a tourist and hadn't checked any of that out. Also, wouldn't it have been cheaper to rent an apartment in town than a dilapidated farmhouse in the middle of nowhere? This all seemed silly conjecture though. We didn't know the Shipleys, the owner, or this tenant who was going to have quite a shock when he returned home tonight. Still, my imagination ran wild with thoughts of insurance fraud.

By this point, the fire had been reduced to smoldering wood. The structure itself was still standing, although there were sections that had been chopped open to give access. Firefighters swarmed around the barn, and I squinted as a dark shape separated from the smoke, moving over toward the pumper truck. I'd seen enough of the human-shaped shadows over the last year to not doubt that I was looking at a ghost—and that I was probably the only one who could see the specter.

Oh no! Had the tenant been in there? Or was this ghost one that had been haunting the farm for decades?

"When was the farm originally built?" I asked the deputy, thinking it was possible that over the last hundred years or so, there might have been an untimely death and thus a spirit hanging around the old barn.

Deputy Raine held up his hands. "Early last century, I think. The Shipleys have farmed here since around nineteen-twenty. Before then, the land was part of some other farm—probably the Fisher farm or maybe the Schillers who used to own the land the lodge now occupies."

The shadow moved from the pumper truck back near the barn, circling around to the side and passing right through one of the people battling the blaze. Nineteen twenty. There was a good chance over four or five generations that someone had died on the property. Although, from my very limited experience and knowledge, a person didn't have to die in a location for their spirit to haunt it. Heck, Holt Dupree was down in Atlanta right now haunting the pro football team he'd been recruited to just before he died. This ghost could be some long-dead Shipley who refused to leave their beloved farm.

The specter didn't move like an elderly person, though. Not that I expected a ghost to be limping around, complaining of arthritis in his hip, but I got the feeling this shadowy figure wasn't the spirit of someone who'd been particularly old.

"Did any of the Shipleys die young?" I asked. "A farming accident, maybe? Or a car accident? Or maybe someone was murdered?"

Because, once again, in my very limited experience, murder seemed to be a good reason for a deceased person to stick around.

Deputy Raine jerked his head to stare at me in surprise. "Murder? No. Why would you ask that? They all died of natural causes. The living ones left town once the farm went up for auction—well, all except for Luke. He's a ski and snowboard instructor, last I heard."

Luke Shipley. I made the connection, thinking of the blond who Madison was so flustered over. What had made him stay when the rest of his family had left the area? It must have been difficult for him to remain in town, knowing the farm his family had owned for generations had been bought and was rented out by an absentee landowner. Or maybe not. Maybe Luke didn't care one bit about the old family farm and just stayed because this was where friends, family, and the mountains he'd probably grown up skiing were.

The firefighters were continuing to get the upper hand with the smoking barn when through the cluster of vehicles came a huge white SUV. Behind the wheel was a pale thirty-something year-old woman with lots of dark eyeliner and burgundy hair piled up on top of her head.

"Skis and poles in the back," she shouted as she pulled up next to us.

Judge Beck glanced down at his phone. "This must be Evie."

"It was nice meeting you," I said to Deputy Raine before I stopped to think that it wasn't really that nice to meet someone at what might be an arson. The deputy nodded and wandered over to stand near his car. I glanced at the ghost once more, then grabbed my skis and passed them to Judge Beck who was loading our gear into the back of the SUV.

We climbed in the backseat, and Evie took off. It took us about twenty minutes to wind around the mountain back to our lodge, and the driver talked the entire ride. I learned all about the Shipley family, how they'd had horses, cattle, and poultry until they just couldn't pay for the place anymore. According to Evie, a man named Bajaj had bought the place at a foreclosure auction, not a tax auction as the deputy had said. Bajaj had bought the place sight unseen through an agent, and, according to Evie, had never stepped foot in town, or possibly even the state, to see his new acquisition. I encouraged her monologue with the occasional question and lots of approving noises and discovered that she thought Luke was a hard-working, nice young man, even if he flirted with every woman on the slopes. According to Evie, that was the best way to get tips, and Luke was known to be saving so he could eventually buy back the family farm.

She glanced at Judge Beck in the rearview mirror as she mentioned the tips. The judge was ignoring her and reading e-mail on his phone. I bit back a grin, knowing he'd tip her twenty percent whether she flirted or not, because that's what he did. And I knew from watching him with Madison's friend's moms that Judge Beck was completely oblivious to women flirting with him.

"Who's renting the farm now?" I asked her. "There was an SUV in the drive, but nobody seemed to be home. Honestly, the place looked vacant to me."

Evie nodded. "A man named Kent Banner. He moved in a few months ago and doesn't really come into town. The farm's off the main road quite a bit, but I like to drive past the farm five or ten miles and hike, and I only ever see his vehicle there. Seems to be a private, unfriendly sort of guy. I know he and Cheryl have gotten into it a few times."

Cheryl? Getting into it with a man renting a neighboring dilapidated farmhouse? That struck me as being just as odd as the cheerful activities director being a volunteer fire-fighter.

"Has anyone ever died there?" My mind kept returning to the ghost. I got the feeling he wasn't young, but not old either. And he was definitely male. I didn't sense anger or any sort of emotion from the spirit, but then again, he'd been pretty far away when I'd seen him, and there'd been no way to get closer without interfering with the firefighters.

My question got Judge Beck's attention. He did a double take from his phone and shot me a puzzled smile, but didn't say anything.

"People die everywhere," Evie said cheerfully. "I wouldn't be surprised if some great, great grandparent croaked in one of the bedrooms ages ago. Or if fifty years ago someone lost a child birthing at home. Why? Did you see a ghost?"

Had *she* ever seen a ghost? I examined Evie's expression through the rearview, wondering if she was joking or serious.

"I did see something around the barn," I said, deciding to take her seriously. "But with the smoke and the spray from the hoses, it might have been nothing."

Evie's pencil-thin, black brows wiggled at me. "Or it might have been something. I wonder if a bear got that tenant. That would explain why his SUV was in the drive-way, but he wasn't home."

"There are lots of reasons why a man might not be home

with his car in the drive," Judge Beck pointed out. "Perhaps he went out to dinner with a friend or went for an evening hike. He could have returned just as we were leaving."

"Or he could have been killed by a bear while he was out hiking." Evie seemed almost hopeful, as if she were really excited at the prospect of the poor man being mauled by local wildlife.

"Is that a common occurrence around here?" Judge Beck asked. "People being killed by bears?"

"Nope, Crow Creek is a squeaky clean, wholesome, and safe town. No shootings or stabbings, no drugs, and definitely no bear attacks." Her voice was cheerful, but there was an edge of sarcasm to it. "But there's a first time for everything, you know?"

I thought of the ghost. "Yes, there *is* a first time for everything."

Evie fell strangely silent for the rest of the drive. She pulled up in front of the lodge and popped the lift gate on the SUV, wishing us a lovely evening and hoping that we enjoyed the rest of our vacation as Judge Beck slid the skis out and I grabbed the poles. We watched as she drove out of the parking lot.

"What's this about a ghost?" the judge asked as we lugged our gear inside.

I didn't want to tell him. Few people knew about the strange ability to see ghosts that had come following my cataract surgery, and I wasn't sure I wanted to count the judge among those who I'd confided in. I trusted him. He was my friend, and my feelings for him were steadily heading into the more-than-friend territory, but I didn't want him to know *this* about me. I'd already confessed to knocking Doug down and my less-than-stellar skiing abilities. It was one thing for him to think I was a klutz; I didn't want him to think I was crazy.

"Nothing." I smiled and shook my head. "It was dark and there was a lot of smoke from the fire. I thought I saw something, but it was probably nothing."

It wasn't nothing. But I was here on vacation. I was here to ski, not to sleuth. So I put the ghost out of my mind and followed the judge up the stairs to our suite, where after a quick shower, I collapsed on my bed and fell into a blissful sleep.

CHAPTER 4

*W*e were up early the next morning, Madison and Henry not the slightest bit tired or sore from their playing at the terrain park the night before. We ordered breakfast in the room, and just like Judge Beck, I made the mistake of checking my e-mail.

The judge's e-mail sent him back into his bedroom with an annoyed grunt to log onto his laptop. Mine had me phoning the office.

"Kay! Gosh, I didn't mean for you to have to call me back. It's not an emergency or anything."

It probably wasn't an emergency, but I'd felt guilty leaving Molly behind to deal with all the skip traces and investigative work with so little experience under her belt. While she'd picked it up quickly and was solid on the routine stuff, there was still much to learn.

"It's no bother. Let me get my computer, and then I'll see if I can help." With a sigh, I opened up my laptop and connected to the lodge internet. "Go on." Madison edged up behind me, obviously curious so I set the phone down. "You're on speakerphone, Molly. Madison is here with me."

"Hi Mads!" Molly called out. "Kay, I'm so sorry to disturb you on vacation like this. I just wanted to get your input before I typed all this up for J.T. to review."

I completely understood. Molly was new, and outside of a month doing skip traces, this was her first time working on an actual investigation. Plus, this was for a new client, and I knew she was nervous about getting everything right.

"I've got your e-mail and I'm pulling up the attachments now," I told her.

Madison leaned in as I opened the pictures. There was one of a wrecked car nose-down in a ditch. Another showed a semi towing a flatbed trailer with a piece of heavy equipment on it. Other pictures were of a bent and scraped guard rail, debris, and both tire and scuff marks on the road. I glanced over at Madison, wondering if she should be seeing this. There weren't any pictures of the injured, but it was still disturbing to see the damaged vehicles. Although Madison was a new driver at sixteen and perhaps she *should* see how horrible a vehicle accident could be.

"The driver of the car died in the accident," Molly recapped. "His fiancée hired us to check into it. The tractor-trailer driver was unhurt. The police say it was the car driver's fault, that he drifted across the yellow line."

"Hmmm." I zoomed in on a few of the pictures, looking at the scrape marks. "Any witnesses?"

"Just the tractor-trailer driver, although a few cars were on the scene immediately afterward. There's a hill there, so the first driver on the scene saw the car in the ditch and the tractor-trailer slowing on the shoulder when he topped the hill."

"The fiancée thinks the tractor-trailer drifted across the line instead?" Madison asked, her face grim as she looked at the pictures on my screen.

"Yes," Molly replied. "I don't blame her. There were no

other witnesses. Maybe the semi driver didn't realize that he'd drifted or maybe he's lying because he doesn't want to admit to causing an accident that took someone's life."

"Or maybe he's telling the truth," I pointed out. "The police report said the load had shifted and that two cables bolting the backhoe to the trailer were snapped."

"The police investigators and the driver both say that happened in the course of the accident. That the car hit the trailer in the center section and that is what caused the cables to snap and the load to shift."

I nodded. "Type all that up and make a note for J.T. to see if the sheriff's department did an accident reconstruction. The load may have shifted and caused the trailer to drift, but if that happened, I'd expect the trailer to have jackknifed. I'd also have expected the damage to be down the whole side of the trailer, especially toward the back. It's just that one spot in the center."

"Got it. Thanks, Kay. Go back and enjoy your vacation. I'll try not to bother you again."

She disconnected, and I closed out my e-mail with Madison still hovering nearby.

"Do you think the semi caused the accident?" she asked.

"No, but the client is paying for us to be thorough. She shouldn't have to live with a bunch of 'what ifs' clouding the memories of her fiancé." I smiled over at her. "J.T. will need to do a lot of research on the truck and how the load was secured. He may even ask to have the client pay for a second accident reconstruction—one by an independent third party."

She glanced over at the bedroom where her father was tapping away on his laptop. "Will you follow-up with Mr. Pierson on it? Maybe do some research of your own?"

"No." I closed the laptop lid and slid it away. "J.T. managed his business just fine before I came along, and he'll certainly survive me taking one week of vacation." I followed her gaze. "He's trying, Madison. He doesn't want to be glued to his laptop the whole week. Just let him have a little time in the morning and in the evening to check in. Unlike me, he doesn't have a J.T. at his office to pick up the slack."

She nodded. "I know. I just…there were so many vacations where Dad seemed to spend more time working than with us. Once he even had to fly back home early, leaving Mom, Henry, and me to come back alone a few days later."

I reached out and touched her arm. "That's not going to happen this time. Now, let's get some breakfast before Henry eats all the bacon."

That broke the spell. We ate, drank coffee, and talked about which resort we were going to go to today. Half an hour later, Judge Beck came out of the room, and we were ready to go.

Piling skis and snowboards into the back of the SUV, the judge drove the short distance to Aspen. We'd already unloaded and were making our way over to have our badges scanned when I saw a burgundy-haired woman gesturing to me from beside a white SUV.

"It's our Uber driver from yesterday." I put a hand on Judge Beck's arm. "Did you forget to pay her or something?" I teased. "She's waving me over."

"I paid, and I tipped twenty percent."

I stifled a laugh. Of course he tipped twenty percent. "Can you have my badge scanned for me? I'm going to go see what she wants."

I left the judge and the kids in line and snuck under the queue rope, walking as quickly as I could with the huge inflexible ski boots on.

"You're psychic, right?" Evie asked me. "Sensitive to paranormal phenomenon? Did you really see a ghost at the old Shipley Farm? You weren't kidding, were you?"

"What?" It took me a second to realize she meant the shadowy spirit I'd seen at the fire last night. "I'm not sure if I saw a ghost or not. Why?"

I had seen a ghost, but I didn't feel comfortable about strangers knowing about my paranormal sensitivity. I should have just kept my mouth shut last night and not mentioned the ghost I'd seen around the burned barn.

Evie hopped excitedly. "Maybelle told me they found a body in the barn. A *body*! That must have been the ghost you saw."

I shuddered, hoping that the person had been already dead when the fire had started. Had it been the tenant? A vagrant? If the guy leasing the farm had been using it only periodically, then maybe someone else had decided to take advantage of his frequent absences and shack up in the barn rent-free. I couldn't imagine anyone else would have been in the barn, even if they had been deceased when that fire started.

And how *had* that fire started?

"There was a lot of smoke, and all the water from the hoses," I told her, reluctant to admit what I'd seen. "That's probably what I saw—some smoke. We weren't all that close to the barn. Judge Beck and I tried to stay out of everyone's way after we called it in."

"Judge Beck?" Her thin eyebrows rose. "That hottie of yours is a *judge*? Girl, you hit the jackpot there."

Heat flushed up my face at the thought. Even if we stayed just friends, I'd still consider that hitting the jackpot. If that friendship kept going where I hoped it was going, then yes indeed, I would have hit the jackpot.

But I wasn't about to go into the details of my relationship with Judge Beck, even if I was sure what that relationship actually was.

"Anyway," Evie waved a hand, "Maybelle says Deputy

Raine turned it over to a detective, who's tight lipped right now about how the guy died. Might be from the fire. Might be from some gash the first responders said he had on his head. Might be from something else. I'm thinking someone whacked him on the head, then started the fire to cover it up."

"What, no bear attack?" I asked, thinking of her conversation last night.

"Good thinking." She nodded sagely. "It could have been a bear that got him, but if so, then who started the fire?"

There were all sorts of natural causes for a fire—anything from combusting damp hay to faulty or old electrical wiring —but I had to admit, the fire looked doubly suspicious when a dead body got thrown into the mix.

"Maybe the man was battling the fire, got hit on the head by something falling, and died," I said, still trying to find a reason for the death that wasn't a bear attack or foul play.

Evie shook her head. "I think it's more likely we've got an arson and a murder. Exciting, huh?"

I'd be lying if I said "no." A murder and someone losing their property to arson shouldn't be exciting, but it was. Who was the dead man? Had someone killed him, then started a fire to cover up the murder? If Judge Beck and I hadn't taken a wrong turn on the slopes, how long would that fire have burned? Long enough to cover up the fact that someone had been either murdered or mauled by a bear inside the barn? Probably not.

Although, sometimes people got lethal head wounds from causes other than murder.

"Aren't we jumping the gun here? Shouldn't we wait until the coroner delivers a report? And the fire inspector? Maybe the guy was working in the barn and just fell from the loft."

Evie snorted. "Right, then why did the barn catch on fire?"

I held out my hands. "He fell while he was holding a lantern?"

"A lantern? Who the heck uses a lantern anymore? He'd have a flashlight or use his cell phone or turn the lights on in the barn. And there's no hay or straw to catch fire in there. No one's had animals on that farm since the bank foreclosed on the Shipleys."

"An electrical fire then," I suggested, returning to my original idea. "It didn't look like anyone had really been taking care of the place. Maybe the wiring had been chewed up by rodents. The tenant falls and hits his head and faulty wiring burns the barn down. Or, like I suggested before, he was out there trying to put out the fire, and he fell and hit his head."

That last one sounded the most likely, but Evie clearly wasn't buying any of it. "Someone whacked the guy in the back of the head, then set the barn on fire to cover it up. I just know it. Anyway, I'm thinking if we go up there later, maybe you can talk to the ghost and find out who killed him. I know you're on vacation and all that, so how about I pick you up around lunchtime. You'll want to take a break after skiing all morning anyway."

The ghosts I'd seen had never talked to me, but sometimes they did provide me with clues. Not that the police would believe a private investigator from out of state who saw ghosts. Still, it would be interesting to go and see what the ghost could show me, if anything. Even if the ghost didn't show up, I was inquisitive and nosy enough to want to snoop around the burned-out barn. The police here were the experts, and they were more than capable of finding the killer, but I was curious.

Plus, Evie was right. It wasn't like I could ski for twelve or fourteen hours straight, even with periodic breaks. I glanced back at the judge and Madison and Henry in line. Our agenda for the day was skiing then lunch on our own.

Around four, we planned on going back to the lodge to shower, change, relax, then have a late dinner and possibly either go back to the slopes or partake in one of the many activities Cheryl had told us about.

I could squeeze this in. I could totally squeeze this in.

"How about you pick me up here at two, we spend an hour at the old Shipley Farm, then you bring me back?"

Evie grinned and gave me a double thumbs-up. "Deal."

I kinda-jogged, kinda-hopped back to the ticket line in my ski boots, taking my place beside the judge and the kids.

"Who was that?" Henry asked, watching as Evie drove away.

"Our Uber driver from yesterday," Judge Beck answered him. "*My* question is 'what did she want?'"

I couldn't think of any reason why a one-time Uber driver would want to talk to me, so I sort of told the truth. "She said that the firefighters found a body in that barn that burned down last night."

"Wow," Henry said.

"Eww." Madison shuddered. "And you were right there. That's creepy."

Judge Beck's expression was thoughtful. I could practically see his brilliant mind turning as he sifted through his memories of our ride with Evie last night. "She tracked you down, someone she met for all of twenty minutes. A stranger." His hazel eyes met mine. "She's one of those ghost chasers, isn't she? And she thinks *you're* one because you were asking if anyone had died at the farm."

I winced at the barely concealed amusement in his voice. I hadn't believed in ghosts either until I started seeing them after my cataract surgery. Still, it hurt to think that he'd believe me to be crazy, lumping me in the same boat as people who went looking for Bigfoot or thought they had been abducted by aliens.

"I don't know, but I do think she's interested in the paranormal." I chose my words carefully. "She wanted me to come with her back to the farm this afternoon to look around."

"Cool! Can I come too?" Henry asked.

"Surely you're not going to go?" Judge Beck sighed as if he already knew the answer to that question. "Kay, you're a private investigator. You know how this goes. The barn is off limits until the fire inspector can check it out. Even then, that barn's not safe to walk in or around. It could be an arson crime scene—and a homicide crime scene if the fire was set to cover up a murder."

"I'll be careful walking around, and I won't go into the barn itself," I reassured him. "I know to respect a crime scene. Evie wants to see if there are any ghosts there and to look around for clues." I hated throwing Evie under the bus for all this, but it was better than having Judge Beck look at me as if I were one of those tinfoil hat-wearing weirdos.

"It's like *Scooby Doo*," Henry chimed in. "Zoinks. Jinkies. Can I come? I'll be Shaggy."

Did that make me Velma or Daphne? Or the dog?

"And you're going with Evie because…?" Judge Beck lifted his eyebrows, ignoring his son's comments.

I squirmed. "I'm going with Evie because it sounds fun. She's picking me up here at two. By then I'll be worn out after skiing for hours and could probably use a break."

Last night had taught me that daily yoga and my halfhearted attempts of exercise at the gym weren't nearly enough preparation for an entire day on the slopes.

"I don't like the idea of you going off with this woman alone, to the scene of what could be an arson and a murder," the judge complained.

For a second, I was affronted. Did he think I was some helpless damsel? I was a private investigator. I'd been going to crime scenes for almost a year now. I'd even been the one to discover the body at quite a few of those crime scenes. I wasn't some fragile flower who was going to be kidnapped by an Uber driver in broad daylight.

Then I realized Judge Beck wasn't worried about my fragile flower self, he was...jealous? What the heck was he jealous about? He certainly wouldn't want to go ghost hunting from his earlier tone about the subject. I almost offered to have him come along, but then Evie and I couldn't talk candidly about what, if any, specters I was seeing. Besides, I was sure him being left out of the fun wasn't the problem. Or was it? Maybe it wasn't the fact that he was missing out on ghost chasing, it was that I was going somewhere without him.

Huh. How about that.

"We won't be gone long." I jostled his elbow. "I promise to tell you all about it. I'll even perform a dramatic reenactment if we see any ghosts."

He smiled, and it did weird things to my breathing. "In the hot tub," he informed me.

"It's going to be difficult to perform a dramatic reenactment in a hot tub," I complained.

His smile widened. "I'm sure you'll manage. Besides, I seem to recall we had a bet about a bottle of champagne and the hot tub before our evening was eaten up by a barn fire."

I *had* wanted to try out the hot tub outside our room. And after four hours of skiing, I might need to soak my muscles a bit. Plus, I did owe him that bottle of champagne.

"Okay. Deal," I stuck out my hand to shake on it. "Dramatic hot tub reenactment with champagne it is."

"I want to be part of the ghost hunting crew." Henry chimed in.

Madison wrinkled her nose. "Well, I don't. Yuck. It'll be

all wet and charred and stinky. I agree with Dad. We came here to snowboard, not hunt for ghosts."

"It'll just be for an hour," Henry countered as we edged further up to the ticket booth. "Just a quick break from snowboarding. It'll be fun to see some ghosts."

"All we're probably going to see is a bunch of mud and slush, a burned-out barn, and an old house," I told him. "If I see any ghosts, whether it's the murdered man, an old prospector, or some ancestor of the Shipley family who died of old age in his bed, I'll tell you."

I wouldn't tell him, but he didn't have to know that.

"Shipley?" Madison turned to me. "Any connection to Luke Shipley, my...uh, the snowboard instructor?"

I caught her slip and noticed her blush. "Yes, it was his family's farm for generations. It was sold to someone else a few years ago, though."

"Oh good." She blushed again. "Not that it's a good thing another person's barn burned down, or that someone was killed. I'm just relieved it wasn't...you know."

Yes, I knew. An employee at one of the windows beckoned to us and we stepped forward. She scanned our badges, affixed the resort sticker to the front, then gave us papers that showed our instructor for the day as well as when and where we would meet them. I looked at my sheet, seeing that I was due for my lesson with Gus in fifteen minutes.

We headed over to the meeting place, and the judge came along, even though he'd not signed up for lessons. Henry's instructor, Skittles, was waiting for him— a lanky freckled boy who didn't look much older than Madison. With an easy grin and a cheerful enthusiasm, he told Henry they'd be doing jumps and spins by the end of the week. Soon after the pair had left, Luke swept into our midst, blond hair glinting in the sun. The young man scored points by chatting respectfully with the judge before heading off with Madison to the terrain park.

"Are you going to wait around to meet my instructor as well? Just to make sure he knows not to take any inappropriate liberties with me during my lessons?" I teased the judge, who was watching his daughter's retreating back with a slight frown.

"If your instructor looks like Luke, then yes."

I laughed. "If my instructor is that young, there will be no inappropriate liberties on either side."

Gus was in his late forties, according to the information sheet on the wall of the rental store, and the man skiing up to us looked just like the picture. He was tall and fit with close-cropped silver hair rimming the edges of a knit cap. He introduced himself and immediately got down to business as soon as we left the judge and headed toward a small slope littered with fallen skiers and those snowplowing their way with agonizing slowness.

"I'll admit I haven't skied in ages, but I think I'm above this level," I laughed. "We took the Easy Stroll trail last night and aside from a spill right after I got off the lift, I didn't fall."

"I just want to get an idea of your technique and balance before we head up the mountain." Gus gestured toward the beginner area. "Think of it more as an obstacle course."

He had a point. Avoiding the fallen and those hopelessly out of control would be a challenge. I grabbed the J-bar and let it haul me up the slope, Gus falling in behind me. At the top, I waited for my instructor to join me then headed down, managing to avoid running over any of the other skiers.

Gus pulled up beside me, nodding thoughtfully. "Not bad. You've got good balance. Basics are solid. What are your goals for this week?"

"Not breaking any bones? Not looking like an inept skier in front of my friends?" I thought of all the slopes I'd seen on the map. "I used to be able to do some of the intermediate slopes, and I'd like to get back to that level if I can."

A smile twitched at the corner of Gus's mouth. "Those are pretty modest goals, Kay. You've got lessons all week with me. Dream big."

Dream big. I envisioned myself flying down the mountain, wind in my hair, completely relaxed and enjoying myself instead of that feeling of jaw-clenched fear.

"I'd like to feel comfortable going faster. I was always afraid I couldn't stop, that I'd be out of control, so I'd use the entire width of the slope and cut back and forth as many times as I could to keep my speed slow."

He nodded. "That's a good start. Today we're going to do lots of fast-slow transitions to build up your confidence in being able to pull the speed back when you want. Let's stick with that today, and depending on how you feel, we can work on something else tomorrow or keep our focus on speed and control."

I felt a wave of relief at his words. Gus had an carefree confidence about him that inspired trust. I knew he could teach me, that I'd learn under his tutelage. And I knew any criticism he delivered would be constructive. We headed toward the chair lifts, Gus chatting about the weather and asking polite questions about my job back home. We managed to get on the lift without incident and began the trip up the mountain.

I peered down at the people on the terrain park, keeping a tight grip on the bar. Some of the snowboarders were doing amazing tricks on rails and jumps, as were a few daring skiers. I spotted Henry with his red striped helmet and bright yellow-and-red jacket zoom up the side of a half-pipe, teeter on the edge, then fall back and slide down on his rear, all while his instructor cheered and shouted instructions and encouragement.

Off to the side near the tree line, Madison sat on the ground next to Luke, their snowboards attached to their feet, up on their sides in front of them. Madison jumped up, pointing her board down the fall line to gain speed as she headed toward a set of boxes. Luke watched her for a few seconds, then took off after her, his board up on its edge as he cut across the slope.

By the end of my lesson I was feeling tired, but I continued to ski for another few hours just to practice what Gus had taught me. I still wasn't fast, but as I went back and forth down the slope almost perpendicular to the fall line, I worked in a few sweeps where I let my skis point more downhill, keeping my weight heavier on the downhill ski and shifting it to my heels to bring the skis around. Fast. Fast. Fast. Slow. Fast. Fast. Fast. Slow. It was exhilarating, and by the afternoon I felt far more confident, and absurdly happy.

After a quick lunch, I grabbed my shoes from the locker, putting my ski gear inside, then jogging back out and over to the pick-up/drop-off spot to meet Evie. She was there early, so I climbed in, grateful for the warm interior of her vehicle and the heated seats.

I didn't notice until I was in the car that there was another woman with Evie. She looked to be in her seventies and was tan as a walnut with a royal blue beret perched with a jaunty angle on snow-white bob.

"This is Maybelle," Evie explained as she pulled away. "When she heard about the ghost, she just had to come."

"I was going to go out there anyway, because who can resist an arson *and* a murder?" she cheerfully informed me. "Then when Evie said you'd seen a ghost…well, wild horses couldn't keep me away."

"Maybelle?" I turned in my seat to see her better. "You're the 911 operator?"

"Yes, I am. It's the best job in the county." She reached up and adjusted her hat. "What do you do? Evie said you're here on vacation with some good-looking judge."

"And his two children," I added, just so she wouldn't get any lurid ideas about what Judge Beck and I were doing when we weren't skiing. "I'm a private investigator." I winced at their obvious excitement at that. "I haven't had my license very long, though. Before that, I did skip-tracing."

That hadn't been for very long, either. Good grief, had it really been less than a year? It seemed like I'd been working for J.T. for ages, my life before quickly receding like the view from a rearview mirror in a speeding car.

"It's wonderful to have an expert along," Evie said, obviously undeterred by my caveat. "We're just amateurs when it comes to crime, but we do watch a lot of shows."

"*All* the *CSIs*," Maybelle chimed in.

"*Law and Order*," Evie added.

"And stuff on YouTube, especially that good-looking Gator man." Maybelle fanned her face.

I couldn't help but laugh. "I work for him. J.T. 'Gator' Pierson. Wow, I didn't think anyone outside Locust Point watched his YouTube channel."

My announcement had both woman in a frenzy of excitement. Evie pulled over after nearly taking the SUV into a ditch.

"You're Kay Carrera!" Maybelle clapped her hands together. "Evie, we have a celebrity in the car."

"Can I get your autograph?" Evie opened the glove box, nearly taking off my knees in her haste to pull out a piece of paper and a pen. I ended up signing my name on an old oil change receipt while the two women recited all the episodes I'd been in on J.T.'s show.

"You solved the Holt Dupree murder." Evie clasped the oil change receipt to her chest. "*And* you see ghosts. It's like we're long-lost sisters."

"All three of us," Maybelle agreed.

I wasn't sure how to take this sudden fandom. "Uh, thanks? Are we going out to the barn?"

"Yes! Of course!" Evie stuffed the oil change receipt down the front of her shirt and pulled back onto the road.

The barn was a mess of soaked, charred timber. The fire inspector and the police must have finished their crime scene work because the tape surrounding the scene only said "caution." I stood on the outside of the bright yellow tape, peering into the barn. It was dark, thin rays of light striping the inside of what was left of the building.

"Here." Evie handed me a pair of low-power binoculars.

There were the remains of what looked to be an ancient piece of farm equipment inside along with a few melted plastic tables—the kind I'd seen used in church potlucks and yard sales.

"See any ghosts?" Evie said in my ear.

"No, but why were there a bunch of plastic tables set up in the barn?" I could see if they were stacked against the side, the barn used for storage, but these were standing in what had probably been rows before the powerful fire hoses had blown them askew.

Maybelle took the binoculars from my hands and looked through them. "Huh. He probably used them for the drugs."

"What?" I exclaimed.

"Drugs," Maybelle repeated as Evie nodded knowingly. "I heard through the rumor mill that the old Shipley farm was being used to break down and repackage drug shipments. Heroin or something. No one is supposed to know, but a man with the DEA spoke to the sheriff about it a few weeks ago."

"You never told me *that*," Evie exclaimed, shooting her friend a disgruntled glare.

Maybelle waved a hand. "I thought it was all horse

phooey, and so did the sheriff. There haven't been truckloads coming up and down this road. No planes landing in the fields. I would have thought there would have been more action if Kent Banner was running some kind of drug operation at the old Shipley farm."

I didn't know much about drug trafficking and distribution, but Maybelle did have a point.

"Kent Banner was the tenant, right? Maybe he was setting up the tables in preparation for a yard sale," I suggested. "Or he was planning on having a barn dance with a potluck dinner."

Maybelle snorted. "A yard sale way out here? That's almost as funny as the idea of Kent Banner hosting a dinner and dance party. The man hardly ever came into town, and when he did, he was downright grumpy."

Evie nodded. "He was grumpy when he was here, too. Nearly shot Cheryl Fisher's head off a few weeks after he moved in. Don't think she's ever forgiven him for that."

"He *shot* Cheryl?" I couldn't believe she was so casual about such a thing. "Evie said they'd had a run in, but not that Kent Banner shot at Cheryl. Why wasn't he arrested?"

"Probably because Cheryl shot back at him." Evie shrugged. "People around here don't generally involve the police unless blood is spilled."

Yikes. "Any idea why the pair of them were shooting at each other?"

"Cheryl was on the property. She's been hiking across the old Shipley farm since before the foreclosure. If the guy didn't want anyone cutting across his fields, then he should have put up notices."

I winced, thinking how things might have gone very differently if the judge and I had skied up to the house and asked for help. Would we have gotten shot at as Deputy Raine had cheerfully implied might have happened?

"Do you know for sure that the body in the barn was this Kent Banner? The tenant?" I asked, looking once more through the binoculars into the barn.

"There was positive ID from the coroner," Maybelle told me. "That's all I heard as of this afternoon. No cause of death yet, although from what the buzz around the station is, it could be a couple of things."

I remembered Evie telling me of a head wound, although I was sure the body had enough burns to hide other injuries from the naked eye. Remembering something else, I turned to look at the small SUV, still parked in the driveway. The other tracks had been completely obliterated by the fire trucks and other first responder vehicles, but they'd been there. Had they belonged to the killer? Or a mail delivery person? Either way, I'd need to remember to tell the deputy about them, or whatever detective was assigned to the case.

"Let me take a look in that barn," Maybelle said, extending a hand for the binoculars. I gave them to her, although there wasn't much to see—at least from this vantage point.

So far, I hadn't seen any signs of the ghost. I left Maybelle and Evie and wandered toward the tenant's vehicle. It was a recent model Jeep Liberty, dark green with fat aftermarket tires. I looked through the windows and saw an empty energy drink bottle in the cupholder and a few pieces of junk mail on the passenger seat.

"Any word on the cause of the fire?" I called back to the two women.

Maybelle passed the binoculars to Evie and headed toward me. "Nothing official. Bruce is leaning toward arson. He definitely said there was gasoline involved, but he hasn't come out and said if it was just an accidently tipped over gas can or a deliberately tipped over gas can. He'll probably have his official report in by tomorrow morning."

"Bruce Zostara is the fire marshal," Evie called out as she peered through the binoculars. "He's also Maybelle's second cousin on her mother's side."

Small towns. Everyone was somehow related to someone else, it seemed.

"Whoever killed the guy did a horrible job of covering it up," Maybelle went on. "The dead guy was smack in the middle of the barn by one of those melted plastic tables. The fire was started out near the front here. You'd think if a murderer wanted to cover up their nefarious deeds, they'd douse the body with gasoline and start the fire right on top of him. Am I right, girls?"

Evie and I murmured our agreement.

I stepped away from the SUV, walking toward the house as I thought everything over. A dead man who'd exchanged gunfire with his neighbor and hadn't been exactly loved by the townsfolk. A dead man who may or may not have been murdered—because in spite of Evie's convictions, I still had a reasonable doubt. A fire that was likely to have been deliberately set.

Was this a really inept murderer trying to cover up his crime or a series of horrible accidents? I wasn't sure which was true, but I was definitely intrigued by the whole thing.

I climbed the front porch of the house as Evie and Maybelle continued to look through the windows of the Jeep Liberty. Had the police searched the house? Would the owner fly in from Florida? Did Kent Banner have any next of kin who would be out to sort through and collect his belongings?

Just then, I saw a shadow out of the corner of my eye. I paused and watched as it slipped from the house and moved purposefully toward the barn. He seemed in a hurry and anxious, and he carried something in his arms. A box? Or a large sack? The shadow paused in front of the drive. From the position of his insubstantial body and head, I got the impression he was looking down the driveway toward the road.

Irritation. Anxiety. A sense of urgency.

I walked over, trying to see what he would have been looking at from his vantage point, and the other two women followed me, Evie walking right through the shadowy form.

She shivered and wrapped her arms across her waist. "There's a draft. No! It's a spirit. A ghost has passed nearby. Maybelle, did you see anything? Kay?"

I shook my head, unwilling to out myself just yet.

Expectant. The ghost was waiting for something? Was it the killer? Had he met the man in this driveway? What had been in the box he'd been carrying?

Maybelle moved so that she was standing right next to the ghost. Lifting both hands to the sky, she wiggled her fingers, humming something under her breath. "I feel something close by. I feel a presence."

While Maybelle was working her mojo, I watched the shadow extend his arms along with whatever he was carrying. The box vanished and the ghost lowered his arms. He'd given the box to someone. His killer? *What was in the box?*

"He's nervous. People are watching him. He had secrets he kept, things he didn't want anyone else to know about," Maybelle announced dramatically.

I turned to her in surprise, because that was the exact impression I'd gotten from the ghost. Was Maybelle truly sensitive? It seemed wrong to doubt her when I'd been seeing ghosts for almost a year now.

Plus, if the place *had* been used for some sort of drug operation, then no wonder the man living here had been suspicious and wary.

"Do you feel anything, Kay?" Evie whispered to me as she stared at Maybelle in reverent awe.

I glanced at the ghost, who strangely had put his hands on his hips and was once more gazing down the driveway toward the road. "There does seem to be a presence," I admitted, torn between wanting to keep my paranormal sensitivity a secret and letting these women know what I was seeing. It would be wonderful to tell someone who would believe me, someone who could actually sense what I was sensing. Daisy knew, but at least one of these women was experiencing something similar. It would be so nice to have a shared experience with someone.

The ghost turned from the driveway and began to walk back to the house. Letting my guard down, I turned as well and watched him enter through the solid wooden door.

Maybelle dropped her hands to her sides. "He's gone. It was definitely Kent Banner. I met him once at Whole Foods in the produce section and recognize his energy. We argued over eggplant."

"You argued about eggplant with the ghost?" Had there been eggplant in the box the ghost had been carrying? What was so important about eggplant that Kent Banner's spirit would include it in his ghostly activities?

"No, before he was a ghost. When we were in Whole Foods. I'd seen him here and there around town before, but that was the first time we'd spoken." Maybelle's lips thinned. "He's a very grumpy man."

"Kay also sensed the ghost," Evie jumped in before I could inquire further about the eggplant incident.

"I saw a shadowy figure here in the driveway. I think he was giving a box to someone," I confessed.

"A box of drugs?" Evie squealed. "It's true then. I'm sure one of his drug cartel contacts killed him and started the fire. It was probably because he was going to snitch on them for a reduced sentence from the DEA man. Or maybe he'd been skimming drugs to sell himself. Or stealing some for personal use."

"Or it was a box of eggplant that he was giving to a friend," I suggested, now completely obsessed with the idea of eggplant.

"If he was dealing drugs or involved in their distribution, there should be some hint of that around here," Maybelle said. "Anything in the barn was probably burned up aside from those melted tables, but there could be stuff still in the house."

"I'm not breaking into the house," I protested. There was no way I was going to do something illegal. The thought that I'd need to call Judge Beck from jail and ask him to post bond for me if I was caught was enough of a deterrent.

"We can peek through the windows!" Evie immediately started toward the house. Maybelle and I followed. The windows I'd tried to look through last night had been covered with thick sheets of blackout fabric or paper, but I hadn't looked in *all* the windows.

Evie took the windows on the porch and Maybelle hopped up and down, trying to see through the higher-up windows on the right side of the house. I went around back, remembering the footsteps that had led from the back porch to the rear of the barn where the stables were. This afternoon, those footsteps were mixed in with those that were most likely mine and the judge's from last night, along with a few more sets that were probably the firefighters or the deputy. Trying not to step in any of them, I crunched through clean snow and onto the porch.

The back door was locked. Not that I intended to trespass, but I figured there would be no harm in cracking the door open to take a peek around while remaining on the back porch. That wouldn't technically be trespassing, would it? The four windows along the porch, just like the others, were covered in the blackout fabric. I inspected them carefully but couldn't see around the edges. The paint on the windowsills was chipped, the wood gray and spongy with rot. Examining the edges, I saw that the glass on one of the windows had cracked around a small hole. It wasn't big enough for me to risk sticking a finger in, but a pen from my purse fit through nicely.

With the care of a woman who didn't really want to lose her pen, I gripped the end, wiggling it back and forth through the hole until I managed to catch the blackout fabric enough to push it aside. I couldn't see much, but I could tell I was looking into a large kitchen with an old farmhouse table in the middle of the room and a battered electric stove on the other side. The table was filled with boxes and what looked to be hundreds, if not thousands, of small plastic baggies. I could make out knives, spoons, and what looked like a postage scale. A small appliance sat on the counter by the stove, too far away for me to clearly make out what it was. A bread machine? An air fryer? Taking my phone from my pocket, I snapped a few pictures of what little the opening in the curtain had revealed.

"What do you see?"

Maybelle's hissed words made me jump. The pen slipped from my hand to clatter to the floor inside the house. The black fabric slid closed, leaving a small opening that gave a tantalizing glimpse of the edge of the kitchen table.

Drat, I liked that pen.

"Here." I showed the two women the pictures I'd taken, and they angled their heads, squinting as if that would somehow reveal more than the hastily snapped photos.

"Drugs." Maybelle announced. "It's just like in the *CSI* shows. Boxes, baggies, and even a scale to weigh the powder before he bags it."

"Guess the DEA guy was right, and the sheriff wasn't,"

Evie added. "Case closed. Kent Banner was involved with some bad people, and one of them killed him and burned down the barn to hide the murder."

Maybelle murmured her agreement, but I wasn't completely convinced. As they drove me back to the slopes, I thought about the items on the table and all the perfectly innocent reasons Kent Banner might have for weighing, boxing, and bagging non-illegal things in his kitchen.

Some of which might have included eggplant.

CHAPTER 5

*M*aybelle and Evie dropped me off with half an hour to spare until the judge, the kids, and I were set to return to our lodge. I got in a quick trip down one of the bunny slopes, working on my turns, keeping my weight downhill, and planning my path to keep my speed at a comfortable level.

The kids were sweaty, snow-covered, exhausted, and full of smiles as we piled our equipment into the SUV. The judge made an excellent executive decision, and we picked up pizzas, salads, and garlic bread so we could relax and eat in the rooms.

Housekeeping had cleaned up our breakfast mess, made the beds, and had the suite sparkling clean. I felt a pang of guilt as we dragged wet boots and skis across the carpet to set out on the back porch. Damp coats draped across chairs, and the dining room table instantly became covered with pizza boxes and bags of food.

"Dibs on the shower!"

Henry dashed into the room he shared with his father. I

heard the door to the adjoining bathroom slam and nearly laughed at the dismay on Judge Beck's face.

"Do you want to use ours? I can wait, and I'm pretty sure Madison wants to eat first."

"Mmrf," Madison mumbled, half a slice of pizza crammed into her mouth.

The judge hesitated, then took me up on the offer. I pulled a piece of sausage, mushroom, and green pepper out of a box and watched Madison eat like she'd been on a desert island for the last week.

"I'm guessing you didn't have lunch?"

She shot me a guilty look. "I did have lunch. With Luke."

"So, there wasn't a whole lot of eating involved?" I was sure Madison was too busy flirting to do more than pick at her food. Plus, she'd probably been concerned about dripping ketchup down her shirt or having a piece of spinach stuck in her teeth.

She blushed and shrugged. "He's really hot. And he's a great snowboarder."

"And he's in his twenties," I reminded her.

"Twenty-one. That's only five years older than me. Lots of women date men five years older than them."

"Not when they're still in high school." I pointed my slice of pizza at her.

She shrugged. "I'm just having fun, Kay. I promise I won't do anything stupid."

"I know you won't." I smiled, reminiscing about when I was in high school. "There's nothing wrong with having a crush on an older man. When I was your age, I used to get all starry-eyed over Burt Reynolds."

She grabbed her phone and typed, then peered closely as she scrolled through some pictures. "Okay. He's pretty cute. What's with the mustache, though?"

I took a bite of pizza. "It was the seventies. All the men had mustaches. Some women did too."

Her head shot up, then she laughed. "Right. So how was *your* day? Did you see any ghosts at the burned-out barn?"

"You'll need to wait for my dramatic hot-tub reenactment to find that out," I teased. "It seems that the fire marshal is leaning toward arson as the cause of the fire, and although there's no official word yet, the two ladies I was with seem to think the fire was set to cover up a murder. They believe the man was involved in a drug distribution ring, and that his life of crime caught up with him."

Madison nodded, digging in the bag for a slice of garlic bread. I had a feeling that poor salad was going to go into the fridge unopened.

"I can see that," she said. "Drug cartels need a safe place to cut the product. An old farmhouse a few miles outside of Aspen would fit the bill."

I eyed her with surprise. She sounded as if she were an expert on the subject. "You really think so? I always assumed any break-down and repackaging would take place in the cities, close to the dealers."

"Oh, it does, but it's been cut two or three times before the suppliers in the cities cut it down yet again for their dealers. The stuff that comes across the border is usually pure," Madison told me. "One ounce of pure gets cut with powdered milk or laundry detergent or cornstarch, and that one ounce becomes a pound. It's easier to cut it when it's already here than to try to smuggle the larger bags into the country."

"How do you know this?" I didn't suspect Madison of having firsthand experience with drugs, and I was hoping she didn't know these things because of a friend.

"School. HBO. And Kaitlin's dad is a DEA agent."

That set my mind at ease, although I was now a bit

curious about what she was watching on HBO. "So, there wouldn't need to be truckloads of drugs coming in?" I asked. "But they would need a decent-sized facility to break stuff down, and I assume they'd need trucks to get the stuff out."

"Depends on if they were just breaking it down there or storing it as well." Madison shrugged. "Guy comes in with a duffle bag full of pure. They've already stored the additive powder, baggies, and everything there that they picked up at Walmart or had delivered from online shopping. Either a group comes in to do the work, or the one or two guys who live there do it themselves. If the drugs are safe there, then they may just send them out a bit at a time. If not, then a dozen cars spread out throughout the week should be able to get it out of the barn and where it needs to go."

There were baggies, boxes, and a scale right there on the kitchen table. And if the man had gotten a sizable shipment to break down, he could have used those tables in the barn.

"You're scaring me, Madison," I teased. "Actually, you'd make a good detective, you know?"

She grinned. "Maybe. Kaitlin's dad says there are a lot of behind-the-scenes jobs at the DEA where people trace money and banking data and basically do internet surveillance. It's like putting all the pieces of a puzzle together. I think it would be a cool job. Or maybe I could work for the FBI."

"Sweetie, you could work anywhere you want."

It was true. The girl was smart and personable. She had good grades and judging from all the SAT prep she'd started a few weeks ago, her scores were going to be excellent. Plus, I knew her dad would use his influence and every bit of pull to make sure his daughter got her foot in the door with any school—and any career—she wanted.

"I can't be a racehorse jockey," she shot back. "I'm too tall and I can't ride a horse. I'll never be a pro-golfer, or a tennis player, or a soccer player. So, in reality, I *can't* work anywhere I want."

"But you've got potential for a college scholarship in softball," I pointed out. "If sports are what you want to do in life."

"A scholarship is a far cry from playing professional fastpitch." She laughed. "You know, I think my softball skills may work in my favor for any job opening in the FBI. Don't they have a softball team? Or is that just on television?"

"I've got no idea." I gave her a quick hug. "Your dad is hoping you go into law, but I think he'd accept FBI or DEA agent as a reasonable second choice."

"What do *you* wish I'd do for a career, Kay?" Her hazel eyes met mine, and I caught my breath at the affection in her face.

"Whatever brings you happiness. I want you to enjoy your job, even if every now and then it sucks. I want you to have friends you love and who love you. I'd like you to have a special someone in your life that can be your partner, who will be the one you love with all your heart and soul."

"Get married and have babies." She grinned.

I smiled back. "Although I love the idea of eventually getting to cuddle your son or daughter, sometimes life doesn't work out the way we want it to. And occasionally people decide that being a parent isn't something they want to do."

Madison's smile faded. "I'm sorry, Kay. Ms. Daisy told me that you and your husband had wanted children."

I smoothed back her hair, surprised to realize that my infertility was no longer the open emotional wound it had once been. Maybe because all my friends who'd had children were now empty nesters, and I no longer felt the reminder with each birthday party, football game, and graduation. Plus, any lingering sense of loss had completely faded now that I had Madison and Henry at our house every other week.

Perhaps it was because I considered them mine. Not *mine*, in reality, but mine in my heart. And they lived in my house where I got to pretend to be a sort-of honorary aunt.

"We did want children, and we tried for a long time. When we found out what we'd have to go through for a slim chance of having a child of our own, we considered adopting. Then Eli and I sat down and had a very serious discussion and realized that in our years together, we'd built a life we loved. His job was incredibly demanding, and I really enjoyed my career. If we adopted, I'd need to quit my job, or we'd need to hire a nanny. We decided that maybe God had something planned for us other than parenthood." I smiled over at her. "I cried some over the next few years. I doubted our decision at times. But I'm not unhappy with how my life turned out."

"Did you have nieces and nephews?" she asked.

I shook my head. "Eli and I were both only children. But I promise you I got to spoil a lot of my friends' children over the years."

"Plus Mr. Eli had his accident." Madison frowned as she did the math. "If you had adopted, you would have had to take care of him as well as a ten or eleven-year-old kid. That would have been hard."

"It would have been, for me as well as for our adopted child. And I can imagine it would have been very frightening for him or her to almost lose a father like that."

Madison paled and shot a quick glance into our room where her father was showering. "I don't know what I would have done if that had happened to Dad. He's so strong, so smart. He's…he's kinda my rock, if you know what I mean. I love my mom just as much, but Dad…it's different."

"I know exactly what you mean." The thought of Judge

Beck nearly losing his life, of surviving, but never quite being the same again, of having to give up his career—it terrified me. I'd seen what Eli had gone through, and I wouldn't wish that on anyone.

"Ms. Daisy didn't have children either," Madison pointed out. "And neither Ms. Suzette nor Ms. Olive. And neither do the Larses."

"But the Burking family at the end of the block has six children. They're making up for the rest of us." I forced a smile, happy to be back on a less emotional train of thought. "I didn't mean to make you sad or think about scary things. I just wanted to let you know that you can absolutely have a wonderful and rewarding life without children."

Madison pursed her lips and nodded. "I don't know if I want kids or not. I think I do, but not for a long time." Then she reached out and punched me lightly on the shoulder. "And you're not exactly child-free, you know. You're stuck with Henry and me, whether you want us or not."

I caught my breath and blinked back a sudden rush of tears, thinking that she couldn't have said anything better.

"If you haven't realized it yet, I love you and Henry very much. Even when you all move out, and your dad marries again, I'm going to still be there for you and Henry like a crazy fairy godmother that you can't get rid of."

Madison tilted her head, her expression quizzical. "Kay, sometimes you are a total doofus, you know that?"

Before I had a chance to answer her, Judge Beck emerged from our bedroom, dressed in clean clothes and rubbing a towel over damp hair. Madison skipped in past him, and I heard the bathroom door shut.

"Is Henry still in there?" The judge frowned toward his bedroom.

"Yes. Which means you have a chance to grab a few slices of pizza before he swoops in here and devours it all."

We ate, and relaxed, me grabbing my shower after everyone else had finished. I'd expected the kids to head out back to the lodge's slopes, but they showed no signs of budging from the couches and the television. It was amazing to think two high-energy teens would be tired after a day of skiing, but they were clearly worn out.

"Is it hot tub time?" Henry asked once the sun had set and the lights on the slopes had come on.

I thought about the bottle of champagne I had chilling in the fridge, then exchanged a quick glance with the judge.

"It seems hot tub time is going to be a family activity tonight. Rain check on the champagne?" he asked.

I nodded. "Rain check. I should have expected the kids would want to see my dramatic reenactment."

"Ooh, that's right!" Madison jumped to her feet. "I'll get on my swimsuit."

Less than ten minutes later, we were all in the hot tub, and I was putting on a show. It was less dramatic reenactment and more of a campfire-esque spooky story with me playing the parts of three women and a ghost.

"Maybelle said the ghost had secrets that he didn't want revealed to anyone," I said, leaning in toward my rapt audience.

"That's the whole idea of secrets," the judge drawled. "You want them to remain...well, secret."

"Hush." Madison splashed water at her father. "Let Kay finish the story."

"The ghost was nervous," I intoned. "Afraid."

"Afraid of the person he gave the box to?" Henry asked. "Or was the ghost afraid of you three?"

"Just afraid in general." I had the impression that the ghost was concerned about someone discovering what he was doing—and most likely what was in the box.

"After the specter handed the box off to an invisible

person, he vanished. Poof!" I shot my hands out for emphasis, inadvertently flinging water at the others. "That was the last we saw of him."

"Did Ms. Evie see the ghost or just Ms. Maybelle?" Henry asked, his eyes huge.

"They both sensed a presence. Evie felt an unnatural chill—"

"Probably because it was twenty-five degrees out today," Judge Beck interrupted.

"Dad!" both kids shouted.

The judge leaned back and made a zipping-his-lips motion, although said lips were clearly biting back a smile.

"—and Maybelle felt the emotions of the ghost," I finished, mock-scowling at the judge.

"What did you see, Miss Kay?" Madison asked.

I lowered my voice, again leaning forward. "A shadowy figure emerging from the house and moving to stand in the driveway, looking down toward the road."

The judge grinned, clearly not believing me, but enjoying the show. Madison looked as if she were unsure if I were serious or not. Henry gobbled it all up as if my tale were the gospel truth.

"Unfortunately, the ghost did not reveal what exactly happened to him on that fateful night to cause him to lose his life." I waved a hand for emphasis. "Was it an accident? Or was it foul play?"

"Foul play," Henry chimed in. "Definitely foul play."

"I'm voting foul play as well," Judge Beck added.

"Me too," Madison said. "Especially if the guy was working for a drug cartel."

The judge frowned at her. "Where did you get this drug cartel notion?"

"Kay and I talked about it earlier," Madison smugly informed him. "The rumor in town is that he was cutting heroin in the barn. Kay saw a scale and little plastic baggies when she peeked through the window in the kitchen, so it totally fits."

I bit back a smile, letting the attention shift to Madison. "It's true. I took a few pictures with my cell phone. It did look like he was set up for some sort of production stuff in that kitchen. There was even some kind of appliance on the counter—an air fryer or something."

"Ooh, we should zoom in on the picture and see if we can tell what it is!" Henry squirmed with excitement. "On the laptop's bigger screen, I'll bet we'll be able to see it better."

"It could be the big clue that solves the case," Madison said. "We can take the information to the police. They'll catch the killer. We'll get certificates or something thanking us for our help."

"Maybe they'll give us a key to the city," the judge said, playing along. "Make us honorary deputies."

"And when they catch the bad guy, he'll say that he would have gotten away with it if it hadn't been for us darned kids," Henry laughed.

"Darned kids and two darned adults." Judge Beck reached out a wet hand to ruffle his son's hair. "You watch too much *Scooby Doo.*"

"There's no such thing as watching too much *Scooby Doo,*" I informed him.

We didn't stay in the hot tub for much longer since the kids were eager to solve the mystery and earn the accolades of the local police department. We rinsed off, dressed in our pajamas, then the kids and I sat down at my laptop while the judge checked his e-mails.

"I'm not sharing my key to the city with you if you're not going to help," I called after him.

He laughed. "You three be the Scooby gang. I'm a judge. I have to recuse myself from this whole proceeding."

That was nonsense, but I didn't challenge him on it. We'd have fun figuring out what the appliance was on the counter of the kitchen, and he could get caught up on work.

"There." Henry pulled the picture up on the laptop that he'd transferred from my phone. He and Madison stared at it, enlarging it and zooming in to the point where it was nothing more than blurred pixels.

"It's probably a bread machine," I repeated what I'd thought earlier. "Or an air fryer."

"Wait." Henry's fingers flew over the computer. "I've seen this before."

"You've seriously seen this appliance before?" Madison eyed her brother. "Seriously? An appliance?"

"I knew it! It's this." Henry spun the laptop around to show Madison and I a store listing for a food dehydrator. It looked exactly like the appliance in my picture, including the small silvery logo at the bottom that I'd been unable to quite make out through the tiny peephole I'd used in the kitchen window.

"A dehydrator?" I had a lot of kitchen gadgets, but I'd never felt the urge to get a food dehydrator. Maybe if I'd had a love of homemade apple chips, but I wasn't much for dried fruit beyond adding it to the few recipes I had that called for it.

But the question wasn't what I would do with a dehydrator, it was what in the world a reclusive single man living in a dilapidated farmhouse would do with a dehydrator. Was he prepping for the zombie apocalypse? Did this item have something to do with the argument he'd had with Maybelle over eggplant?

"Drugs." Madison nodded knowingly. "Some drugs you make into a paste after you cut them, then you form them into bricks for sale. The bricks have to be dried. I'll bet a food dehydrator would make quick work of that."

I shook my head, still amazed at what she'd picked up from HBO and her friend's father.

Drugs. Everything was pointing that way. Evie and Maybelle were most likely right, and Kent Banner had lost his life due to his illegal dealings, the fire set to cover up the murder. I briefly wondered if there hadn't been a fire, how long the body would have laid there undiscovered? Yes, Judge Beck and I would have knocked on the door for assistance, but when no one answered, we would have called for an Uber, not gone out to search the barn.

If there had been no fire, then someone may have gotten away with murder. Although given the current lack of hard evidence or clues, someone *still* might get away with murder.

CHAPTER 6

"Oh. I thought...." Madison looked at her sheet, disappointment written on her face.

We'd gotten up early, eaten a light breakfast, and headed straight to the slopes. After a downhill run together, we were once more picking up today's assignment sheets. I glanced over Madison's shoulder and saw that she'd be with "Red" Douglas today, not Luke as she'd obviously expected.

I'll admit I was a bit relieved. Young love was a beautiful thing, but I was a little uncomfortable with Madison's crush on the attractive blond man.

"Red's a great instructor," the woman at the window informed us. "You'll learn a lot. I wouldn't have been able to do a 50-50 without his help."

I had no idea what a 50-50 was, but obviously the kids did.

"A 50-50?" Henry looked at Madison's ticket. "Can I have Red teach me next time? I'm still trying to get up the side of a half-pipe without falling on my butt."

"Then you're probably not ready for a 50-50." Madison

rolled her eyes and shoved the ticket in her jacket pocket, obviously still unhappy about her instructor assignment.

Luke had been on her sheet as of yesterday. As thrilled as I was that she had Red teaching her instead, I wondered why the sudden switch had occurred. Had Judge Beck started to worry about Madison's crush and asked for her to have a different instructor? Had Red pulled some strings?

"I thought you liked Skittles," the judge said to his son.

"I do. I'm just teasing." Henry wrinkled his nose. "I think the problem is with me, not the instructor. Snowboarding is hard. I thought it would be just like skiing."

The judge reached out and patted Henry's shoulder. "You can always switch back to skiing if you want."

"No way!" Henry declared. "I'm going to be doing those 50-50s by the end of the week if I have to spend the whole night on the slopes to do it."

"Is Luke out sick today?" Madison asked the woman at the ticket window, her mind obviously still on the object of her affection.

"He had something come up last minute." She nodded to Madison. "Trust me, you'll be thrilled with Red as an instructor. They're both really good, but in my opinion, Red's got a better way of explaining things."

"Oh, it's fine." Madison smiled, quickly hiding her disappointment. "We're here all week. I'm sure Luke will be able to teach me some other time."

We each went our separate ways with our instructors. Gus and I continued to work on controlled speed downhill, and I diverted the topic of conversation to the events of two nights ago whenever we were on the lift. Unlike Maybelle and Evie, Gus wasn't a gossip. He shrugged and told me that Crow Creek didn't have any more of a drug problem than any other small town. He'd never met Kent Banner, never heard any rumors about what he was or wasn't doing at the old Shipley Farm. He expressed concern about the fire and bland sympathy that the man had died, but that was it.

The third trip up the mountain, I gave up and let him steer the conversation back to skiing.

"You're getting much more confident," he told me as we got ready to get off the lift. "I think it's time to move on to the black diamond slopes."

No, it wasn't. "I don't think I'm ready for that."

We got off the lift, and Gus waited until we'd come to a stop to ask me why.

"They're really steep, especially out west here. And..." I eyed the billboard-sized map looming beside us. "I don't do moguls."

"We can work through the steep sections together," he insisted. "Remember, you've got the ability to slow down if you're going too fast. Let yourself fly a little, then come back. Little bursts of speed that turn into longer and longer bursts of speed. You can do it."

"Maybe tomorrow." I was such a chicken.

"Okay," he relented. "Let's talk about the moguls then. What don't you like about them?"

I laughed. "That I can't get through them? I always end up stuck in between the moguls and falling down. There isn't enough room to get back up without taking my skis off, and people are flying around and past me, almost running me over because I'm flat on my back in between the moguls where they can't see me. Then once I get my skis off, there's the walk of shame out of the mogul field before I can put them back on and try to get down the mountain. Moguls are horrible. I hate them."

My voice grew louder and more insistent as I spoke, and Gus held his hands out as if he were worried I might smack him with a ski pole.

"Whoa! Okay, okay. I think you're approaching the mogul

fields wrong. That's a technique issue we can work on, for one. Plus, now that you're more comfortable with speed, you've got a better chance of getting through one without getting stuck. You've got to be moving to handle moguls. Slowing down is what gets you in the ruts."

"I can't go fast through those things. I have to go slow enough to see where I'm going." I didn't want to do moguls. Couldn't we just stay on the intermediate slopes and keep working on the fast-slow stuff? No black diamonds. No moguls.

No broken legs. No getting run over by someone who didn't see me. No embarrassing myself.

Gus eyed me for a long second before speaking. "We can tackle a small mogul field tomorrow, planning our strategy before we head down. You can follow me, so you don't have to worry about plotting the course. Let's work on this tomorrow."

"Let's not," I snapped.

An awkward silence stretched out between us, and I felt guilty that I'd gotten worked up and taken my fear and frustration out on Gus. He hadn't pushed me any harder than I wanted to go. He'd never pushed me outside my comfort zone. This wasn't about him; it was about me.

Did I want to test my limits? Did I want to see if, with proper instruction, I could conquer things I hadn't been able to do before? Did I want to even *try*?

Or was I happy staying where I was? Sixty wasn't old, but it sure as heck wasn't young, either. I wouldn't be able to shrug off a bad fall like I might have forty years ago. I didn't want to get hurt. But I also didn't want to avoid doing the things I wanted because I might end up injured or embarrassed. Heck, I could break my leg tripping on my front porch step, and that was a whole lot less fun than flying down a black diamond slope and weaving my way through a mogul field.

"Think about it," Gus broke the silence with a gentle tone. "Sleep on it, and let me know tomorrow. I think you can do it, Kay. I've watched you ski, and I wouldn't suggest something unless I believed you had the skill to accomplish it."

I nodded, and we set off down the intermediate slopes, me going a little faster with each turn and holding the speed for a longer period of time before I slowed myself down. By the time we'd reached the bottom of the mountain, I was ready for a break. Today hadn't been as physically exhausting as yesterday, but emotionally I felt drained.

As we made our way across to the chair lift, I saw the two women waving me down at the end of the line.

Gus looked at his watch then chuckled and glanced over at the women. "How did you meet Maybelle and Evie? I should have known you'd been talking to them when you started asking questions about what happened at the old Shipley Farm."

"The judge and I were there when the barn was on fire," I told him. "We'd been skiing, the Easy Stroll trail and took a wrong turn. We were heading to the farm to ask for a ride, saw the fire, and called it in."

"Ah. That explains a lot. Evie and Maybelle tracked you down to do some sleuthing with them."

I nodded. "I know I'm on vacation, but I can't seem to resist a good mystery."

"Well, our lesson is over for today anyway." He waved toward Evie and Maybelle. "Go see what today's gossip is and solve our small-town crime. Tomorrow we'll talk some more about your goals for the week and whether you want to tackle moguls or not."

I grimaced, thinking that maybe I could call in sick tomorrow and skip the moguls. Gus skied away and I headed toward the lift line where Evie and Maybelle met me halfway.

"Fire marshal says arson!" Maybelle announced. "Gasoline as an accelerant. They found the melted remains of a plastic gas can. Looks like someone dumped it out over the front walls, threw the can into the barn, then lit it all up."

Arson. And that meant murder was more likely than an accidental death.

"Come with us." Evie bounced on the balls of her feet. "We're going to try to communicate with the ghost. Maybelle brought some sage and a crystal ball."

Normally I would have doubted such a thing was possible, but my friend Olive was sensitive, and sometimes the spirits would agree to speak to her. I was intrigued that Maybelle might have a similar talent.

"Why do you want to talk to Kent Banner's ghost?" There had to be more interesting ghosts to talk to in Crow Creek besides a criminal that had met a violent end.

"He might be able to tell us who killed him." Evie put a hand on Maybelle's arm. "Maybelle's brother's step-cousin-in-law overheard the sheriff and the detective talking at the diner this morning over their pancakes. He heard them say that Kent probably died of smoke inhalation."

I recoiled, horrified that the man had been alive when the fire was set and not dead from the head wound the first responders had seen. If the killer had only checked before trying to cover up what he thought was a murder, then maybe Kent Banner would be alive today.

Or maybe he'd be just as dead and with two head wounds instead of one. If the man truly was involved in drug trafficking, then it wasn't likely the head wound was an accident. Whoever did this wanted him dead, whether that was by blunt force trauma or smoke inhalation was probably unimportant to the killer.

"The buzz is that someone hit Kent Banner over the head, then panicked and started the fire when he was out cold, thinking he was dead."

"Wait." I was completely confused at this point. "I thought one of the guys in the drug distribution killed him? On purpose. Murdered him because he was skimming or something."

"The sheriff is still poo-pooing the whole drug thing." Maybelle rolled her eyes. "They're getting a warrant to search the house, but the judge is out on a hunting trip and won't be back until tomorrow to sign off on it."

"Isn't there another judge available?" Crow Creek was a small town, but surely the county had more than one judge?

Maybelle shrugged. "Yeah, but he said the detective should wait and get permission from the owner of the farm first, so they're waiting for the other judge to come back."

"Kent Banner wasn't a local," Evie tried to explain. "There's no family breathing down anyone's neck about his death. It's not like there's any real urgency on this. Besides, no one's gonna break into the house or anything."

"They aren't?" I shook my head, frustrated with this whole thing even though it wasn't my town or my case.

"I know. It bothers me too," Maybelle said. "If this guy was involved in drug distribution, who's to say his buddies won't be back to search the house and burn it down as well?"

I thought on that. "If they wanted to search the house, then they probably would have done that before starting the fire. Professional criminals wouldn't be so sloppy. Killing someone, setting a fire, then having to return to the scene because you forgot to search the house for the drugs? It doesn't sound right."

"But what if it wasn't a drug cartel co-worker that killed him?" Evie wiggled her eyebrows. "He and Cheryl have exchanged gunfire. What if they came to blows, and he accidently fell and hit his head when they were fighting? Cheryl is a volunteer firefighter. She'd know how to start a fire."

I thought about that for a second. "Wouldn't Cheryl look beat up if she'd fought with someone?"

Maybelle shrugged. "Cheryl's pretty tough. She cleans up nice, but I'd be willing to bet she could hold her own in a fight. Besides, she might not have bruises on her face."

It was a good point. I'd briefly seen Cheryl when we'd come through the lobby last night, and she'd looked just as well-put-together as always. But with pants, long sleeves, and a high turtleneck shirt, there was no telling if she had bruises or cuts. Plus, I hadn't been close enough to get a good look at her face. Makeup could hide a lot, especially at a distance. I made a mental note to try to get a better look at her this evening when we went back.

"This is why we have to talk to the ghost," Evie insisted. "Maybe the killer is a horrible criminal, but maybe it's Cheryl? Or someone else. We have to know, and I'm sure even as unpleasant as Kent Banner was in life, his ghost will want us to bring his killer to justice."

"Ghost testimony isn't going to convict someone," I reminded them, just in case they hadn't realized that fact about our judicial system.

"Oh, I know, but I'll bet the ghost can lead us to clues. If he tells us there's a threatening letter in the kitchen junk drawer, or in an old coat pocket, then we can tell the detective where to search when he gets his warrant."

I guessed there was nothing wrong with that. And there was nothing wrong with me leaving the slopes for a few hours to participate in a séance at the old Shipley farm.

"Just give me ten minutes to change out of my ski boots and grab my purse," I told the ladies.

They promised to pick me up by the ticket booths. I skied over to the lockers where we'd stashed our stuff to put on footwear more suitable to walking. Then I pulled my phone out to text the judge and let him know where I was going.

The road to the old Shipley farm was getting pretty familiar. I looked out the window and up at the winding snow-covered trail along the backside of the mountain that the judge and I had taken that night, then at the narrow track where we'd made our wrong turn.

"That's going to be a popular add on to the trail," Maybelle told me as she followed my gaze. "Rocky's been working on it for months now."

"It crosses a section of the old Shipley farm," Evie added.

I frowned, wondering if Rocky had leased the land from the owner, or bought it outright.

"Luke Shipley wants to buy the entire farm back," I mused. "Would *he* be open to leasing that section to Rocky for the extra trail?"

"Probably," Evie said. "That kid's been saving every dime to get the farm back in the family. He'd be glad for it to generate a little income right off the bat." She snorted. "Luke would probably lease it to Rocky for less than he's currently paying."

"You know, Luke's got the twenty percent to put down and the bank okayed his loan," Maybelle added. "I don't think Mr. Bajaj wants to sell though."

"He probably bought it as a tax write off," Evie chimed in. "It's been vacant pretty much since he bought it—until the last couple of months anyway. He can't be making any money on it."

I shook my head, amazed at how much these women knew about the goings-on in this town. As interesting as this all was, though, it didn't give either Rocky or Luke motive to kill a tenant—to kill Mr. Bajaj, maybe. Kent Banner, no.

We pulled up next to Banner's vehicle, still parked exactly where it had been the night of the fire. As I watched,

Maybelle and Evie found a level spot and started setting up candles, and little bundles of sage resting in saucers. A shadowy figure materialized by the porch, floating a few inches above the ground and leaning back against one of the supports. I got the feeling it was watching us, intrigued by what was going on. The other two women continued lighting candles and incense, seemingly oblivious to the fact that the ghost they were hoping to summon was only twenty feet from them.

Once everything was lit, Maybelle raised her hands in the air, tipping her head back as she'd done before. I wasn't sure if it was as a result of her call or curiosity, but the shade did detach from the porch and drift over to the circle of candles and sage.

"Who murdered you, Kent Banner?" Maybelle intoned. "Give us a name. Tell us who ended your life."

The ghost floated around the edges of the circle. Evie shivered and looked around excitedly. Maybelle remained absolutely calm and continued to entreat the ghost to reveal his killer.

I wasn't sure if Maybelle heard anything. I didn't, but I did see the ghost turn and float away toward the barn. My experience was that ghosts sometimes showed me how they died, or where evidence was, rather than communicate with whispered voices or words written in a steamy mirror, so I followed the shadowy figure, leaving Evie and Maybelle behind.

Instead of slipping into the barn, the ghost led me around to the back of the burned building where a separate building jutted out, forming what looked to be stables. He hovered, his insubstantial form sliding back and forth between the stalls. The stables weren't in any better shape than the other buildings. Gray paint peeled from weather-swollen boards. A few half-doors hung open, and some were missing entirely, giving me a view of dirt floors, ancient hay, and some large brown lumps that might have been old horse poop. The ground outside the stables had been churned up by all the firefighters since the building was within feet from the back of the barn where the fire had occurred. Other than some scorched siding, this building had been left unscathed by the arson. I took a few steps closer, trying not to slip on the icy puddles of frozen water from the hoses. The ghost hovered near one of the stalls, then slipped into the barn through an open sliding door.

I watched the shadow, trying to stay outside of the barn both for safety reasons and because this was still a crime scene. The ghost seemed very preoccupied with the plastic tables. Was the spirit going through the motions of his normal day? Because he didn't seem to be reenacting his death at all. After a few laps, the shadowy figure vanished into another section of the barn, leaving me to wonder what, if anything, I was supposed to glean from this.

I nearly shrieked as the shadow suddenly materialized next to me. Clasping a hand over my chest, I watched it slide toward a collapsed portion of the stable area, then bend down and flick something toward me.

I jumped, alarmed and unsure what the heck had just happened. Then I bent down to see what the ghost had flung my way.

It was a badge, partially melted with the lanyard mostly burned off. It had landed upside down, showing me nothing but the clear white plastic of the back, so I used the tip of my boot to flip it over.

The Foxdancer Lodge logo stared up at me. Even melted, I could still make out the bar code. Kneeling down, I took a few pictures of the badge, zooming in to get a better look at the number on it.

I didn't touch it. The ghost might not be able to smudge

any latent fingerprints, but my picking the badge up certainly could. Leaving it in the snow, I went back around the barn to find Evie and Maybelle both excitedly talking about the ghost.

"Did you see the ghost, Kay?" Evie asked me. "I felt it. Twice."

"Kent Banner didn't speak to me." Maybelle's voice was husky with disappointment. "I felt him near, but he either couldn't communicate or didn't want to."

"Do you know who the detective is working this case?" I asked, avoiding answering Evie's question about the ghost. "There's something around back behind the barn that I think the crime scene people missed."

Maybelle's eyes got huge. "The murder weapon? Another body? A kilo of drugs?"

"It's a badge," I told her. "It might be nothing. I just wanted to let whoever is in charge of the investigation know."

"I'll call it in," Maybelle said, pulling her cell phone from her parka pocket and moving away.

"It could have been Cheryl's," Evie told me. "She's a volunteer firefighter, and she works at the lodge."

That had been my thought. It definitely could have been something she dropped while fighting the fire, but why would she have had her badge outside of her protective gear? I would have assumed she'd either pulled it off before suiting up or tucked it inside.

I shrugged. "Or it could have just been someone coming out to look after last night's fire. Maybe someone from the lodge wanted to see what happened. I mean, it's not far, and from what I've heard, this sort of thing doesn't happen often in Crow Creek." Although if that were the case, then why was the badge melted?

"It doesn't," Evie agreed. "Maybe it's Luke Shipley's badge. I'm sure he was pretty shaken up to hear the barn burned."

I remembered that Luke had called off unexpectedly today. The explanation would have made sense, except for the fact that the badge was melted, and the lanyard burned off. That led me to believe it had either been here prior to the fire or during it. I couldn't think of a good reason for Luke to have been here before.

"Is Luke Shipley a volunteer fireman?" Because that would absolutely explain it if the badge was his, although just like with Cheryl, I'd still wonder why the badge had been on the outside of his fire suit.

"No, he's not," Evie told me. "He's worked as a ski and snowboard instructor since he was in high school but has never been a volunteer with the firehouse."

"Bruce is on his way," Maybelle said as she rejoined us.

"Bruce the fire marshal?" I knew this was a small town, but I was surprised the fire marshal was also the homicide detective.

"No, Bruce Burnside. He's my third cousin's brother-in-law's sister-in-law's brother," Maybelle informed me.

That wasn't a surprise. It had quickly become clear to me that Maybelle was in some way related to everyone in town. Knowing that I had plenty of time before I'd need to meet the judge and the kids, I helped Evie and Maybelle gather up the séance supplies, then waited for Detective Bruce Burnside to arrive.

CHAPTER 7

*W*e waited out front until an unmarked Crown Victorian pulled up and a sturdy man stepped out. Detective Bruce Burnside wore a pair of khakis and a white button-down with a coffee stain partially concealed by a burgundy tie that had white-and-blue diagonal stripes across its wide width. The tie ended a few inches above his waistband.

Maybelle made the introductions, then the detective surprised me by shooing both women away.

"Go home," he informed them. "I'll give Ms. Carrera a ride back to the resort. I don't need the pair of you gossips screwing up the only murder case we've had in years. Go on, now."

Evie and Maybelle complained, but finally complied, Evie pantomiming that she'd call me later. Since I'd never given her my cell phone number, I assumed she would be trying to reach me at the lodge.

Burnside waited until the women had driven away before turning to me. "So, Ms. Carrera, Maybelle tells me that you're a private investigator?" This detective seemed more enthusiastic about that fact than other officers I'd encountered.

"Yes, but I'm not working a case." Hopefully, that would reassure him that I wouldn't be poking my nose around in his investigation. After all, I was on vacation.

Who was I fooling? I would absolutely be poking my nose into this investigation. I was too curious to do otherwise. That's the whole reason I was here, at the scene of the arson and murder, pointing out something that could be a key bit of evidence.

"My family's been in law enforcement since the early twentieth century," Burnside proudly informed me. "Ever since great-grandad solved his father's murder."

If he'd wanted to hook me into a story, he couldn't have done better. "What happened to your great-grandad's father?"

Detective Burnside squared his shoulders and planted his feet, obviously settling in for an epic tale.

"See, great-great-grandad Joe was buried with a wooden head because my great-great-grandma was a good Irish woman, and she wasn't going to let her husband go into the ground without a proper wake, and you can't exactly have a proper wake around a body that doesn't have a head."

This story was worth coming to Colorado alone. I had so many questions. "Had your great-great-grandpa's head been so damaged during whatever had caused his death that his wife couldn't cover it with something? His hat, maybe?"

"Nope, it was 'cause his head was gone. Missing. Never found." Detective Burnside cheerfully informed me. "He was run over by a carriage out by Kelly Junction. A neighboring farmer found him the next day when he was taking his cows to water. Joe's head was gone. Everyone figured a coyote took it or something. Good thing he had his pocket watch on him for identification of the body, although my great-great-grandma probably recognized him by his clothes."

I was completely enthralled, momentarily forgetting about the crime scene right in front of me. A coyote *stole the man's head*? All sorts of gruesome scenes went through my mind about how Joe's head could have come detached, and why a coyote would have decided to take that particular body part and run off with it.

"Anyway, can't exactly have a wake with a headless body, so my great-great-grandma bought a wooden head the general store was using to display hats, then had someone paint Joe's likeness on it. They did a good job from what people said. Looked just like him. He was even buried with the head, because that's only proper, you know."

"And Joe's son found the man who'd run him over?" I asked, assuming that was the part Detective Burnside was circling back to in his tale.

"He did. Stood up on the table beside his dad's body and vowed to catch the killer. Took him the better part of a year, but he solved the case."

I nodded, wondering if they ever found Joe's head, or the coyote who'd stolen it.

"Of course, once he found out, he wished he'd just let it all be buried with Joe. Such shame on the family. Great-great-grandma refused to speak his name for the rest of her life."

I sensed another story but was powerless to resist. "Who was the killer?"

Detective Burnside planted his hands on his hips. "Joe himself, that's who." The man paused a few seconds to let that bombshell settle in. "Seems he'd had enough of his wife and six kids and decided to run off. He knew great-great-grandma would have stomped down to hell and dragged him back if he'd just disappeared, so he faked his death."

"And killed a random stranger?" I asked, horrified.

"Nah. He paid the undertaker a few towns over to let him know when a stranger or a bum with no family died. He went and told great-great-grandma that he was walking into town, that he'd be back around nightfall and not to hold supper for him. Then he got the body, dressed the dead man in his clothes, and left him in the road. Took his head off so no one would know it wasn't him."

This was just as fascinating a story as the wooden head one. Had a passing carriage driven over the headless man, or were those the injuries he'd originally died from? What had great-great-grandpa Joe done with the head? And what did his wife do to him once he was discovered alive and partying it up as a single man?

"Anyway." Detective Burnside waved his hands. "Great-grandpa Buchanan Burnside found his father and brought him back home. Joe spent the rest of his life working the family farm and getting yelled at by his wife. When he died, great-great-grandma didn't bother with a wake since she'd already had one for Joe. There's two graves with his name on them, side by side."

"What happened to your great-great-grandma?" I asked.

"She married again at age eighty-two to a man half her age. She's buried out with his family." Detective Burnside shook his head. "So, Joe's all alone except for that poor sod he decapitated and left in the road. Buchanan was famous all across the county for his detective work. People came to him from all over asking him to sleuth for them, and five years later, he ran for town sheriff and won."

"And the rest is history." I grinned.

Detective Burnside grinned back. "The rest is history. So, Miss Kay Carrera, why don't you show me what you found at this here farm?"

I led him around to the back of the barn. "You don't want to know what I'm doing here, hanging out at a crime scene?"

"I know exactly what you're doing here." The detective chuckled. "Evie and Maybelle dragged you out here to sleuth with them. You and your friend discovered the fire and called it in. You're a private investigator, and your friend is a judge. And Evie claims you're sensitive to paranormal phenomenon."

Word definitely spread fast in the town of Crow Creek.

"I'm sorry to drag you out here, but I saw this and thought it might be relevant to your case." I pointed to the badge on the charred, frozen ground.

Detective Burnside pulled on a pair of gloves, picked up the badge, and slid it into a clear plastic evidence bag before examining it.

"Foxdancer Lodge," he said, which wasn't exactly crack detective work since the name was clearly written and above the melted and burned portion of the badge.

He squinted. "Over twenty-one since there's not a blue line across here. Even though this part's melted, there's enough intact that I'm pretty sure I could see the line if there'd been one."

I resisted the urge to lean over his shoulder. "That's most of the staff and guests, though. It could be anyone's. Maybe even Cheryl since she's a volunteer firefighter."

The detective shook his head. "Cheryl was here that night, but she wouldn't have had her badge on, or outside her suit where it could have gotten in the fire like this. Besides, it looks like this is an instructor's staff badge, not one of the lodge management or help or a guest."

"How can you tell?" This time I did look over his shoulder at the badge.

"The lanyard—at least what's left of it. Instructors have blue lanyards; management has purple."

He was good. I hadn't even noticed the slight difference

in lanyard colors. "That brings the list of suspects down to...."

"Six, since this is a Foxdancer Lodge badge and not one of the larger resorts." He flipped the badge over to see the empty expanse of white on the back. "Course, with all the soot and the heat, the purple might have turned kinda blue. Rocky should know who needed to have their badge re-done. And there might be enough of this barcode undamaged to narrow down who it belongs to."

"It could have been here from before the fire," I pointed out. "As in maybe weeks before the fire. With the first responders here, and all the equipment, it could have been dragged up from the dirt into the open."

The detective nodded. "Could be, but I'd still want to know why someone who worked at the lodge had been out here. The farm's not exactly on the main road, you know. And the tenant wasn't known for being hospitable or social."

"Do you think someone from town killed him?" I asked. "There are rumors he was murdered because of his involvement in drug distribution."

Burnside shrugged. "Not sure yet. And just because the tenant didn't socialize much, doesn't mean he didn't have an out-of-town visitor now and then."

"There was no other car or truck on the property, but there *were* fresh tire tracks when the judge and I arrived," I pointed out. "The only vehicle here at that time was that one over there, supposedly owned by the tenant."

He squinted, chewing on his lower lip. "I didn't know that about the tire tracks. By the time I came out, everything was a mess 'cause of the fire. And that wasn't in the report Deputy Raine gave me."

I suddenly felt guilty. "At the time we'd spoken to the deputy, we had just thought we'd come upon a hay fire or electrical fire. An accident. The only reason I noticed the tracks was because we were checking to see if anyone was home to alert them to the fire. At first, we figured the residents were out."

The detective nodded thoughtfully. "That's Kent Banner's vehicle right there. Registered to him and all. According to the DMV, he's got nothing else. Interesting, although it's not going to do me much good with any tracks being driven over by the fire trucks."

I thought of all the people who might have come to see Kent Banner that night, of the ghost handing off what appeared to be a package to an invisible person, of his strange tour of the stables and barn just now, and my mind kept going back to the accusations that the man was involved in illegal activities.

"What do you think about the rumor that the tenant was part of a drug operation using the old Shipley farm to distribute narcotics?" I asked the detective.

He grinned. "Rumors spread like butter on hot toast around here, Ms. Carrera. This guy moves in, rarely shows up in town even after living here for two months. He's reclusive. He's a stranger. He doesn't ski or hike or hunt or fish that anyone can see. He doesn't work the farm he's rented. He covers all the windows with blackout curtains. He gets into an exchange of gunfire with his nearest neighbor over some casual trespass."

I grimaced, seeing how that sort of person would inspire all sorts of curiosity from the locals.

Detective Burnside sighed and slowly shook his head. "There are people convinced the man was a serial killer, that he was conducting unholy satanic rites. I've heard that he had insider knowledge about money or gems, or gold hidden on the property. I've heard he was doing drugs, running a human trafficking ring, spying on us for the Russians."

"Was he Russian?" I asked in surprise.

"Heck if I know, although Banner doesn't seem like a Russian name to me. The guy sounded like a normal ol' American last time I swung by to check out claims that he was building bombs for a planned attack on the ski resort."

"What were all the tables in the barn for?" Surely a reasonable detective investigating claims of possible bomb making would ask the tenant that question.

"Don't know. Man has a right to store his stuff in the barn he's renting just like the rest of us." The detective lifted one shoulder in a shrug. "For all I know, the man was doing mail-order assembly or something like that. I believe a person's got a right to privacy, Ms. Carrera. That's what I told the sheriff when he said some DEA agent called him. Sherriff told them if they got a warrant to arrest the man, we'd help them serve it. Until then, none of us have seen any lawbreaking activity going down here."

I could respect that. "But even though he was reclusive, *someone* from the lodge was here. Maybe they're a suspect. Maybe they can shed some light on who this tenant was and who might want to kill him."

He nodded. "And to be honest, only one lodge employee comes up in my mind as having an obvious reason to be visiting this farm, although I can't imagine him as being the sort to murder someone."

"Luke Shipley."

The detective regarded me with amusement. "You catch on pretty quick, Ms. Carrera. And you've only been here... what? Two days?"

"Three." I pointed to the badge. "You think Luke Shipley came out here and argued with the tenant over...what? I know he was trying to buy the place from the owner, but that doesn't have anything to do with the current tenant. I'm sure he's bitter about his family losing the house, but Luke doesn't strike me as the sort of person who'd take it out on someone who was just renting the farm."

"Like you said, plenty of people in town think Kent Banner was part of a drug operation that was using this place to cut down and repackage heroin before they sent it out for distribution. That upset people, including Luke Shipley."

"The drugs?" I thought about Rocky Forrest and his "clean and wholesome Crow Creek" spiel. Cheryl, too. And I was sure many other people in town were equally frustrated that their perfect Mayberry of a town was harboring a drug operation.

Detective Burnside nodded. "When we asked around, we couldn't find anyone who actually saw anything. Rumors aren't enough to go in for a warrant."

I frowned, wondering if the drugs had gotten Kent Banner killed, or the rumors had. Or maybe shooting at Cheryl had. "Do you think Luke, or one of the residents of Crow Creek, might have decided to take the law into their own hands?"

He shrugged. "I've got a whole lot of things I'm thinking, Ms. Carrera. But then again, I just started investigating this case. No telling what else I might turn up in the next week or two."

"Week or two?" I teased. "Detective, you've got the Burnside reputation to uphold here. I expect you to solve this mystery in the next two days."

He grinned. "The best detective is determined and patient, Ms. Carrera. Now, let me drive you back to your lodge while I try to track down Rocky Forrest and see if someone in his employ can verify who this badge belongs to."

I had the detective drop me off at the slopes rather than at the lodge. A few hours later, I'd had about as much skiing as my legs could stand, so I retreated to the dining area, got a cup of hot cocoa, and positioned myself at a table where I could look out at the skiers. The snowboard park was within clear view, and I watched people sliding their boards along rails, taking jumps, and performing daredevil moves on the half-pipe. Not all the snowboarders were experienced. There were plenty who were doing just as much sliding on their rear ends as they were on their boards.

Out of the corner of my eye I saw someone approach. I turned and watched as Luke Shipley took the chair across from me, turned it around, and straddled it.

"I thought you'd called out sick." I eyed the young man, thinking that he didn't look as if he'd been sick a day in his life.

"I had some personal stuff to do." He scooted the chair in close, his expression serious. "I heard you're a private investigator. I heard you're kinda famous."

I wasn't sure where he was going with this, but I needed to set him straight before he started confessing things to me, thinking we had some sort of attorney-client privilege.

"I'm not famous. I've only received my PI license this year. I was a journalist most of my life and have mainly been doing skip tracing the last year, not investigations."

I didn't tell him that I'd done plenty of investigations on my own without a license. No sense in encouraging him.

"But you know how to investigate things," he insisted. "I heard you solved a big case where a football player was killed."

My mind drifted back to the badge the ghost had thrown at me, and the conversation I'd had with the detective. If Luke had been out at his old family farm either before or after the fire, then he really didn't need me. He needed a different professional.

"If you've done something or think you might be accused of something, then I recommend you talk to a lawyer," I cautioned him.

"I don't need a lawyer." He scowled. "I didn't do anything, I just…think other people might believe I've done something."

"What exactly do other people believe you've done?"

He picked at the laminated tabletop. "That maybe I had something to do with Kent Banner's death. I've kinda got motive. I hated that my family farm had been foreclosed on. The man that bought it has been neglecting the house and barn. They weren't in all that great shape when we lost the farm, and it's getting worse. The roof leaks. The porch is ready to fall down unless those rotted posts get replaced. It all needs painting. Half the barn siding needs replacing. I'm trying to buy it back. I've saved money. I've got preapproval on a loan. I offered the owner a fair amount, but he won't sell."

I felt for the guy, really, I did. Reaching over the table, I patted his hand. "It has to be hard for you to watch the house you grew up in be so neglected."

Eli and I had spent a fortune fixing up our old Victorian, and in the ten years of his disability, all the work we'd done had started to slide into disrepair. Judge Beck's rent paid the mortgage, but even with the raise that came with my PI license, I wasn't able to do much more than fix the urgent stuff. If the furnace went, I'd be in serious trouble.

"The owner doesn't care about the farm and neither did Kent Banner. It feels disrespectful. Six generations of my family worked that farm. There's love in every room of that house, but the owner can't even be bothered to fix the porch. For almost two years, it sat empty. Then two months ago, it's rented out to someone who treats it like a flop house, or a cheap motel he can trash."

"You've seen inside?" I asked, wondering how Luke knew the tenant was trashing the place. With all the blackout sheets, I hadn't been able to see anything beyond that little bit in the kitchen, and I'd definitely tried.

He squirmed. "No. He keeps all the windows covered and won't let anyone in. But I can just tell he's trashing the place. And I'll admit I've been out there, just to check on the farm, for sentimental reasons."

"And you've had words with the tenant." It wasn't a question because I pretty much knew the answer.

"I've spoken with him," Luke said carefully. "But I didn't kill him. I wouldn't kill him or anyone else. I love my home, and I'm sad to see it go like this. If someone had bought the farm, loved it, did their best to take care of the place and work it like it like my family had done, then I think I could move on. I'll admit I'm angry at what happened to a place I grew up at—a place that my family had for generations. But I'm not angry enough about it to kill someone over it."

"Well, motive isn't enough to arrest someone for murder," I told him, thinking of Cheryl.

"Maybe. Maybe not." He looked down at his hands, then back up at me. "Can I hire you? To prove I didn't do it?"

Oh, for Pete's sake. "First, I'm on vacation and only here for a week. Second, I'm not in a position to—"

Luke interrupted. "But you could research stuff. Evie does it all the time, and she's not a private investigator."

"Third, I think you need to let Detective Burnside do his job. You're jumping the gun here, Luke. Let the police work the case, and if you find yourself in trouble, get a lawyer. Not a vacationing private investigator from out of state."

He huffed something that sounded like "fine," stood up, and stormed off, nearly walking into two women who were making their way into the café. I watched him go, thinking that Luke hadn't told me everything, and that he might actually be in trouble.

* * *

"So, how did the ghost hunting go?" Judge Beck smiled over at me as he loaded the skis and snowboards into the SUV.

"The ghost declined to communicate with Maybelle, but his presence was felt." I debated adding in my own observations and decided to remain vague. "It seems the ghost was in and around the barn, especially toward the back where the stables were."

"Exciting. Did he write the killer's name in the soot? Knock over a table and reveal the murder weapon?"

I chuckled. "No. But I did find a partially burned lodge ID, and the detective working the case came out to collect it."

I didn't mention that the ghost had been the one who'd clued me in to the presence of that ID. So, in a sense, he *had* been revealing clues, if not the actual murder weapon.

"Are you and your new friends going back out to do another séance later tonight, when the moon is full, and the spirits might be more communicative?" he teased. "Or will you be joining us in our plans for the evening?"

"Plans?"

"We're going back out on the slopes," Henry shouted from the backseat.

The judge laughed at the expression on my face. "The kids are going back out on the slopes. I'm going to take some painkillers, soak my feet, and lament that my sedentary lifestyle has led to widespread muscle atrophy."

I doubted that. Yes, the judge worked long hours sitting at a desk in front of a computer or stacks of papers, but he also played golf regularly. I guess that wasn't quite the same as skiing, though. I could sympathize. My legs were killing me, and I was exhausted. My daily yoga clearly wasn't the same as skiing, either.

"I might get a second wind after dinner. Not enough of a

second wind for more skiing, though," I added hastily. "There's that lecture at the library I was thinking of attending—the one on the history of the town. Detective Burnside told me an amazing story about his great-great-grandfather faking his own death. I'm hoping to hear other tales of quirky residents from ages gone by."

Judge Beck finished loading the boots and closed the trunk. "Do you mind if I join you? It sounds like a fun evening. Storytime at the library."

I blinked at him in surprise. "Really? I thought you were just going to chill in the suite tonight."

"I can chill at the library, then chill in the suite later." He smiled and went over to get into the SUV. "I'm on vacation. I might as well get in as much scenery, skiing, and culture as possible."

I climbed into the passenger seat. "Better take some extra painkillers then." I'd certainly be downing a few myself as soon as I got back to my room.

The kids chatted excitedly on the way back, reminding me what it was like to be a teenager and full of endless energy. Madison had seen Luke near the ski shop toward the end of the day and was hoping that he'd be teaching her lesson tomorrow, even though she admitted she'd learned a lot with Red handling her instruction. Henry was completely fixated on leveling up his snowboarding skills this trip, where it seemed Madison was at that age where sports were quickly sacrificed for the company of a good-looking boy.

When we arrived at the lodge, I was wasn't surprised to see Detective Burnside there, chatting with Rocky. The man moved fast; I'd give him that.

Cheryl was behind the front desk, giving instruction to an employee. I told the judge and the kids that I'd meet them upstairs, then meandered over and pretended to peruse a rack of brochures. Rocky and the detective went into the gift shop. The lodge owner waved his cashier away and escorted Burnside over to the badge kiosk himself. I watched them, torn between wanting to know whose badge it was at the crime scene and wanting to get a better look at Cheryl.

"Are you going to Peabody Mann's talk tonight at the library?" Cheryl asked, making up my mind for me. "It's a huge hit with residents and guests alike. He's kind of our local celebrity."

I pulled a brochure off the rack and took her opening as an excuse to approach the desk. Cheryl looked immaculate as always, knife-pleat jeans paired with a plum button down, the entire outfit accessorized with delicate gold and amethyst jewelry. She did seem to have on a bit more makeup than usual today.

"The judge and I are thinking about it," I told her, remembering her question. "We're both pretty tired, though. It might come down to whether we're up to driving into town or not."

She grimaced. "The resort van's taking a group of skaters into Aspen tonight, or I'd offer it up to you."

"I can drive them down in Rocky's truck, " the desk employee said with a wave at the red truck parked outside. "Fern said the logo item order came in. I can pick it up then bring them back after the library thing is over."

Cheryl shot her a sideways glance. "Nice try, but I need you working the desk tonight, not running errands. Besides, when have you ever seen Rocky let anyone drive his truck?"

A decal on the truck door was large enough to be identified as the Foxdancer Lodge logo at this distance, but small enough not to scream the advertisement from a mile away. The red truck didn't look all that special, but I understood how people might not want others spilling stuff on the console or screwing up the seat settings.

A red truck had been driving down the road when the

judge and I were deciding to head to the old Shipley farm for assistance, and the logo on the door might have been a Foxdancer Lodge one. But Cheryl lived down that road. She could have a lodge truck of her own to drive back and forth to work.

"Are there other trucks like that one?" I asked. "Do you have a fleet of them or something?"

Cheryl laughed. "Uh, no. There's the one lodge truck, which is pretty much Rocky's personal truck, then there's the van. I'm sorry, Ms. Carrera. If you guys are too tired to drive, maybe call an Uber? I'd hate for you to miss Peabody's talk, but there's no hotel transport available tonight."

Was it Rocky coming down the road that night? Or some other red truck with a different logo on the door? I hadn't been able to see it well enough at that distance to tell.

"We'll probably be okay to drive tonight." I turned back to her and noticed a dark smudge on her jaw, not quite hidden by her makeup. "Are you okay? You've got a bruise."

She lifted a hand to the smudge and looked away. "I got it fighting the fire at the old Shipley farm the other night. Whacked myself with the end of a hose."

It was a plausible explanation. I wondered if any of the other firefighters had seen her prior to suiting up and could verify that her face was bruise-free at that time.

"You're supposed to be wearing a helmet with a face shield," the desk employee chided, giving me another reason to doubt Cheryl's excuse for the bruise.

"Clearly I put it on too late," the woman snapped back before turning to me with a strained smile. "Is there anything else I can do for you, Ms. Carrera?"

A dismissal. Clearly, she didn't want me to ask any more questions about the truck or the bruise. I shook my head and turned away from the desk, wondering whether I should speak to Detective Burnside about my suspicions or not.

Rocky made a beeline for me, intersecting my path before I got to the stairs.

"Bruce says you were the one who found a lodge ID out by the old Shipley farm," Rocky whispered as he caught up with me. "I hope you don't think one of our employees was involved in that arson, or in the death of the man they found in the barn. I screen everyone carefully before I hire them, and honestly, I've known most of my employees my whole life. I grew up here, you know. I'm sure it was just a coincidence that you found a badge out there."

I patted his arm reassuringly. "I feel very safe at Foxdancer Lodge. It never crossed my mind to worry that one of the employees here might have been involved in something criminal."

It *had* crossed my mind. One thing I'd learned way back when I'd been writing articles for the paper was that those who committed crimes weren't always the stereotypical bad guy. I thought of Peony, of Melvin Elmer, of Mayor Briscane. Sometimes the perpetrator was the last person you'd expect to be involved in a crime, especially murder.

"We're all law-abiding citizens in this town, Ms. Carrera." Rocky frowned. "Well, except for Silas McCoy."

I sensed another tale. "Who's Silas McCoy?"

He looked around to ensure we weren't overheard, then pursed his lips together and brought his pinched fingers to his mouth, like he was puffing a cigarette. I hadn't been a complete angel in college, so I got the reference right away.

"He smokes pot? But isn't that legal in Colorado?" I asked, confused as to why Rocky thought that made Silas a criminal. Unless Rocky was one of those sorts who felt that using or distributing marijuana should still be a punishable offense.

"He grows it. He smokes it. He sells it." Rocky scowled. "And he did it before that devil's weed was legal. I won't let him anywhere near the lodge though, so don't you worry about him trying to sell you that stuff or smelling it around here."

I wasn't sure how to respond to that. Pot was pretty far down on my list of concerns. And given that there had just been an arson and a murder fairly close to the lodge, pot should be at the bottom of Rocky's concerns as well. Why was he telling me about the town pot dealer? Was he trying to shift my attention from what had happened at the old Shipley farm to something more benign?

Rocky leaned in, and I did as well. "The badge you found had nothing to do with the fire or the murder. If someone killed that man and started the fire out at the barn, I'm thinking it was Silas. Everyone knew that guy living out there was into drugs. I'm sure Silas didn't like the competition, went out there, and took care of the situation, if you know what I mean."

"Yeah. That might have happened," I responded slowly.

It was a good thing Rocky wasn't the detective here. A small-time pot dealer killing a narcotics distributor? And how would a big-time heroin operation be competition for a local guy growing weed? I wondered if Rocky wasn't doing some wishful thinking here, trying to get rid of two smudges on the town's pristine reputation with one crime.

"I just wanted to reassure you that these sorts of things aren't common around here." Rocky repeated before he headed back to where Cheryl and the front desk clerk were reviewing papers. I watched him go, then turned to see Judge Beck waiting for me at the top of the stairs.

"I was beginning to wonder what happened to you." He took a few steps down to meet me as I climbed. "What did our host want?"

"To convince me that arson and murder are a rarity in this perfect town. According to him, the only criminal they have is a local pot grower, who he totally threw under the bus for the murder and arson."

"Ah, the stoner did it." Judge Beck's blue eyes twinkled with humor. "What did the dead man do to deserve death, steal his party-sized bag of Doritos?"

"Maybe all will be revealed at tonight's talk." I waved my hands in the air. "Accusations. A surprising plot twist. The killer confesses right there in the library next to the self-help section."

The judge grinned as we started up the stairs together. "Given what we've experienced in the last few days, I'd say anything is possible."

CHAPTER 8

*D*owntown Crow Creek was as adorable as the brochures had described it. A huge fountain graced the center of town, blue tinted water spraying from the mouth of a giant mosaic trout into a basin. I paused to dig a penny from my purse and make a wish before tossing it in to join the thousands of coins lining the bottom of the fountain.

"Wishing for another exciting evening minus the arson and murder?" Judge Beck asked.

I wagged a finger at him. "If tell you, then it won't come true."

My wishes were always basic. This time I'd hoped that we'd continue to enjoy the vacation and have a safe trip home. That Henry wouldn't break a leg trying some trick at the snowboard park. That my sore muscles would be ache-free by tomorrow morning when I strapped on skis and faced my fears.

Judge Beck took my arm to stop me, then pulled a coin from his pocket, tossing it in the fountain as well.

"There. If you're going to wish for something, then I should too."

The streets flanking the square had been blocked off to traffic. We continued toward the library past the brightly lit shops bustling with tourists. Everything western themed—the jewelry on display in one window, rhinestone studded boots in another. The shop selling shot glasses and keychains had salt and pepper shakers shaped like bucking broncos and cowboy hats. I eyed them as we walked past, knowing they'd look ridiculous in my antique-filled Victorian home, but tempted anyway.

The library loomed beside an art gallery, its façade a good two stories above the actual building. People milled about the steps drinking hot cider and coffee. A woman dressed as if she'd stepped out of an episode of *Bonanza* handed each of us a pamphlet as we walked in.

We had just enough time to get ourselves a Styrofoam cup of spiced cider before a woman climbed on a makeshift stage and clapped for all of us to take our seats. The judge and I commandeered two of the metal folding chairs midway back and off to the side so we could make a quick exit if the talk proved to be too boring.

I had high hopes as the woman welcomed us and intro-duced Peabody Mann, their local historian. Peabody came on stage with the assistance of a highly carved wooden walking stick, then took a few seconds to put on his glasses and pull out a thick wad of notecards before he began.

I quickly realized why the room was packed. Peabody Mann had a dramatic oration style that truly held an audi-ence captive. As he warmed up with some general informa-tion about the history of the town, I realized that a good number of the attendees were actual residents of Crow Creek. Either Peabody varied what stories he presented, or this was something of a regular social outing for the townsfolk.

The first tale was about the feud between the house of prostitution, which was now a steakhouse, and the church next door, that was still a church. Peabody then talked of a mine haunted by the ghosts of those who had worked there, of a ranch where several famous barrel racing horses had been bred. He told the story of Joe Burnside's faked death, and I laughed at his embellishments on how the missing man's wife reacted to his reappearance.

"You might think a man faking his own death and a long-closed house of prostitution is the extent of our past in the town of Crow Creek, but you'd be wrong," he announced dramatically. "We have a history! A history of fraud, of violence, and most importantly, of sabotage in the awarding of the title of Grand Champion Rutabaga at the county fair."

The fraud turned out to be planted gold in an attempt to sell one of the non-profiting mines just outside of town. The violence was two fishermen coming to blows over who had rights to a trout stream. And the rutabaga sabotage spoke for itself. We clapped enthusiastically when Peabody took his bows and announced he'd be signing his book on local history—which was for sale by the door for the low price of nineteen ninety-five.

"How much of that do you think is true?" the judge asked as we slowly made our way toward the exit.

"All of it, although I'm sure the actual events were less exciting than Peabody's retelling of them." I eyed the man signing books behind the table by the door. "I think a lot happens here that gets swept under the rug. The colorful antics of rutabaga-growing farmers and trout fishermen suit the town PR better than arson and murder."

The judge nodded. "True. I can't say I blame them for keeping that away from the tourists. People flying in to ski, hunt, fish, camp, and hike want a wholesome frontier fairy tale. They don't want to know about murder, homelessness, or addiction. And it's their tourist money that pays the bills for most of these people."

He was right. There was the Crow Creek that the tourists saw, and the Crow Creek that the residents lived in day-to-day. In some ways, the town was just like the façade of the library—two stories taller than it truly was, putting on a false front for those who only wanted to walk by and admire, but not come inside.

What happened two nights ago smudged that image. I looked around, thinking that most of these tourists had no idea what had happened at the old Shipley farm. If anything, they probably just thought a barn had caught fire by accident, and that the town would rally together and help the poor farmer who'd lost at most a supply of hay. They wouldn't know about arson or murder. They wouldn't know about the DEA suspecting this cute little town was being used to move shipments of heroin. People like Peabody, Carol, and Rocky would make sure the tourists never knew. They'd take care of their dirt behind the scenes, where it wouldn't affect the tourist money.

It wasn't a bad thing, but it made me think that Luke wasn't the only one who had motive to kill the tenant at the old Shipley Farm—Crow Creek was a whole town full of people with motive.

We finally made our way up to the table, the judge and I both taking a twenty out.

"I'll buy," Judge Beck told me.

"Then I'll get one for Daisy. She'll get a kick out of it," I told him, thinking it was probably polite for each of us to purchase a book since we'd both enjoyed a talk that had cost nothing.

Peabody Mann gave everyone the same smile, wrote the

exact same sentiment in each book he signed, but when I reached out for my copy, his eyes suddenly met mine.

"You're the detective staying out at Foxdancer, aren't you?"

"Private Investigator," I corrected him. "From a small town just about the same size as this one. We're enjoying our stay."

The edges of his mouth turned down. "Aside from the other night, I hear. I know Maybelle and Evie have been dragging you around the last few days, but you shouldn't pay them any mind. They're always chasing ghosts and stirring up a lot of nonsense out of nothing. The fire was a terrible accident, and so was the death of that poor man. I'm sure he dozed off in the barn, knocked a candle over, and the hay was ablaze in seconds."

What hay? What candle? And *poor man*? From everything I'd heard, no one liked that man—at least not enough to mourn his passing more than what was polite.

"I'll write about it in my next book," Peabody continued. "I'm sure whoever lives there next will talk about seeing a ghost of a man heading out to the barn, candle in hand."

Maybe not candle in hand, but he probably wasn't wrong about the ghost. I mumbled something, the judge and I collected our books, then left. We made it to the street before we started to laugh.

"Poor man. If only he had taken a flashlight out to the barn last night instead of a candle," Judge Beck intoned in an excellent impression of Peabody Mann.

"Maybe if he'd stacked his hay on all those plastic tables instead, the tale would have had a much happier ending." I placed a hand on my heart and shook my head.

"And napping in the hayloft with the candle beside him." The judge shook his head. "If only he'd gone back to bed."

I snorted. "Then the house would have burned instead of

the barn. Dratted candles in haylofts. They caused the Chicago fire and now this one."

It made me wonder how much Peabody *had* embellished the tales in his book. During the talk, I'd assumed the basics had been true, with only a few flourishes for entertainment. But if Peabody was going to change the arson and murder of a narcotics middle-man and turn it into a tragic accident caused by a sleepy farmer with a candle, then there was no telling what had really happened at that mine, trout stream, or county fair.

Judge Beck linked his arm in mine as I wondered if the two competing rutabaga entries had resulted in less hair pulling and more stabbing.

"Want to shop a little before we head back to the lodge?" the judge asked. "I've got my eye on a pair of those cowboy boots."

I grinned as I imagined him in his pristine dark blue jeans and polo shirt, sporting a pair of hand-tooled, pointy toed boots. Would he wear them on the golf course, or just when we went to the local steakhouse for dinner?

"You get your boots," I told him as I steered him to the shops. "I'm going to buy a few gifts to take back home."

"And something for yourself, I hope?"

I nodded, thinking of the salt and pepper shakers. "Definitely something for myself."

I'd left the shop loaded up with magnets, shot glasses, keychains, and several sets of the cowboy hat salt and pepper shakers only to see that Judge Beck was still trying on boots. I waved at him through the glass, then pointed next door, indicating that I'd be at the jewelry store.

As soon as I stepped inside, I realized this was not the jewelry store for me. The necklaces, bracelets, earrings, and rings had actual gems worked into their silver and white gold. It seemed the store showcased local artists whose wares were far outside my budget. The woman behind the counter was helping actual paying customers, so I waved her off with an apologetic smile, telling her that I was just browsing.

Browse I did, as well as drool a little on the glass topped cases. I'd never been one for heavy jewelry with turquoise and coral, but a few of the artists' creations were right up my alley. I made my way over to a case of broaches, thinking that it was a shame wearing pins had gone out of style. I loved having a pretty pin on a scarf or on the lapel of a jacket.

These were especially beautiful; the artist had worked the metal and gems into inch-long replicas of alpine flora. The Hepatica had purple enameled petals, and a yellow topaz center flanked by tiny diamond chips. Spring Snow Flakes had pearled caps and emerald encrusted leaves. The Indian Paintbrush had ruby and garnet flowers curving along a golden stem. I sighed and stepped away, looking at a few sets of earrings in another case. The same artist that had created the pins had clearly designed a few of these. I looked at a pair of Forget Me Not flowers in enamel with topaz centers and made a decision.

Ten minutes later, they were tucked inside my purse, and my checking account was considerably lighter. Hopefully the furnace wouldn't go out any time soon, because I hadn't been able to resist buying them. Madison would graduate in less than two years and these would make a wonderful gift. What better sentiment to give a girl heading off to college and her adult life then these flowered earrings? Hopefully each time she saw them, each time she wore them, she'd think of me and Forget Me Not.

The judge was standing outside the shop holding two giant boot boxes.

"What, you couldn't decide?" I asked as I waved toward his purchases.

"I couldn't resist getting two pairs." He laughed. "One pair is black with silver embellishments; the other pair is brown with black inlaid leather."

"Are you going to wear them to work?" I envisioned the judge with his fancy western boots peeking out from under his solemn black robes.

"I might." He grinned. "It'll be a new style for me. Maybe I'll start talking with a Texas drawl, start addressing everyone as ma'am and pardner."

"I'm sure that will go over well." I laughed.

We walked to the car, then drove back to the lodge in companionable silence.

"Hungry?" Judge Beck asked as we walked in. "Madison and Henry said they were going to grab burgers before they went to the slopes, so we don't have to worry about having to eat somewhere teenager friendly."

Madison and Henry were hardly picky eaters who existed only on chicken nuggets and pizza, so I assumed he meant fine dining with cocktails and wine. The judge did have a beer during our backyard barbeques, but outside of that he tended to stick to non-alcoholic drinks when he was with the kids. I wasn't sure if that was something he'd always done, or if the divorce and custody struggle had made him very careful about any habits that could be used against him. The last few months I'd noticed a considerable easing of tensions between the judge and Heather, though. I hoped that meant they'd made strides in dividing up their assets and agreeing on custody and a schedule for the kids.

"There's only one restaurant in the lodge," I countered. "Does adult dining mean you want to go back out?"

Adult dining. It sounded kind of naughty, like we'd be eating in the buff or watching racy movies.

"I hope you don't mind, but I was thinking of ordering delivery." The judge stopped at the front desk and surveyed the flyers displayed in a wooden rack.

"They deliver fine dining?" I teased.

"I said adult, not fine dining." He shot me an amused glance. "We can get room service from here, or pizza, or Chinese, or Manny's ribs."

"Ribs?" Pizza was becoming a staple at home, and Chinese delivery was a close second.

Judge Beck pulled the flyer from the rack. "Ribs it is. You go on up and get comfortable. I'll order, grab a bottle of wine from the bar, and meet you upstairs."

The man didn't have to tell me twice. I climbed the stairs, exhaustion coming down on me like an anvil. I'd barely had time to change out of my ski clothes before we'd headed to the library, and I was longing for a hot bath. Deciding it would probably take at least half an hour for the food to arrive, I settled on a shower, putting on a set of comfortable pajamas and leaving my hair loose and damp. It might a bit casual for dinner, but we were eating in the room, and it wasn't as if the judge hadn't seen me in my pajamas before. We did live together after all.

Coming into the common room, I was pleased to see that Judge Beck had the same idea. He was wearing pajama pants with small flying tacos imprinted all over them, and a threadbare t-shirt from some bar that had most likely been closed since the last decade.

"Did Madison pick those out?" I asked, pointing to the pajama pants.

"Henry. He's in a taco phase, plus he thought the pun about our cat's name was downright hysterical. He's also in an alien cat phase. Don't be surprised if you see me tomorrow night with laser-eye cats on my pajamas."

I don't know what it was about Judge Beck in pajamas that turned me into a mushy mess. The man looked amazing in a suit. He looked equally amazing in business casual and his weekend attire. But there was something about those baggy drawstring pajamas and ancient t-shirts that did it for me. Add in his mussed bedhead hair and sleepy eyes, and I definitely looked forward to mornings.

Tonight, his hair was neat and his eyes alert, even though he did hide a yawn behind his hand as he picked up two wine glasses from the dining room table and filled them.

"I thought about having the bartender mix up a couple of cocktails for us to start with, but I was afraid I'd be face-down in my ribs snoring away. I might have to limit myself to one drink," he said as he handed me my glass.

"Me too."

I sat down on the sofa, scooting myself sideways so I could curl my feet up under me. Judge Beck sat beside me, then reached out to clink his glass against mine.

"Here's to vacations. May our future be filled with them— at least two each year."

"Agreed." This had been my first vacation in nearly twelve years. Before Eli's accident, his career trajectory had whittled down our available time. Even when he took off for a long weekend, he didn't want to be more than an hour from the hospital. This trip had been such a treat. I might be tired and sore, but I was absolutely enjoying myself. I might have to limit future trips to less pricey locals, but I intended to make vacations a regular occurrence. Maybe I could wheedle J.T. into letting me use his cabin at the lake for a week this summer. From the pictures I'd seen, it would make the perfect getaway.

And I couldn't help but imagine the judge there with me. My cheeks grew hot, embarrassed that I couldn't seem to shake this crush I had on my roommate.

It was more than a crush. And even though Daisy urged me to take a chance and let fate take its course, I was still scared—scared of ruining what we had by pushing things too far. And scared that I'd make a total fool of myself. What if I'd misread his kindness and friendship as something more?

That was me: scared of moguls, scared of taking a chance to see if friendship could be something more.

"I was thinking about going to the lake for a week this summer," I blurted out. "J.T. has a cabin there with a boat for fishing and a couple of kayaks. There's a jet ski rental shop, hiking trails, and a place with ziplines a few miles down the road. It's not too remote, and lots of families vacation there."

"That sounds wonderful." Judge Beck sipped his wine and looked off into the distance. "Henry and I haven't been fishing in over a year and Madison has been wanting to jet ski. We should definitely do that this summer."

We. He'd said we. I stared at his profile for a moment, wondering if I should take this group vacationing thing to mean...something.

There was a knock on the door, and the judge got up while I took a large gulp of wine. *Don't ruin what you have. Just be satisfied and don't go messing up a good thing.*

After paying the delivery man, the judge took the bag over to the dining room table and began to unload the containers.

"Stay right there," he instructed as I started to get up to help him. "I'm serving you dinner. Relax. Drink your wine and get ready to eat because this smells delicious."

The aroma was truly mouthwatering. As the judge filled the plates, he informed me that Manny smoked all the meat himself, and that the barbeque sauce was a recipe that had been passed down from his grandfather. I happily took the plate Judge Beck handed me and dug in. The meat fell right off the rib bones, tender with just the right amount of honey-and-smoke goodness to the sauce. The potato salad was German style with mustard, apple cider vinegar, and chopped bacon mixed in.

"This is just like what my grandmother used to make," I said, pointing a fork at the potatoes.

"Hope you have her recipe," the judge mumbled in between bites.

We scarfed down our food, went for seconds, then finally relaxed back on the sofa. In spite of his earlier statement, Judge Beck did decide to have a second glass of wine. We sat next to each other, our thighs nearly touching. I debated leaning my head over and dozing on his shoulder but didn't want to spill my wine.

"So, tell me about the murder and arson that you and your Scooby gang are investigating? Who are your top suspects?" he asked.

I set my wine on the side table because I needed both hands to check off the list of clues. "So far, all I have to go on is motive and opportunity. Yes, the lodge ID was by the barn, but whoever left that might have nothing to do with either the arson or the murder."

The judge shrugged. "Okay. Then who has motive?"

I snorted. "Pretty much everyone in town. My money right now is on Cheryl."

He turned to me in surprise. "Cheryl? Cheryl-with-all-the-brochures, Cheryl?"

"Yep. She and Kent Banner had a run in that involved a mutual exchange of gunfire. The body had a serious head wound, which leads me to believe there was a fight leading up to the murder/arson. Cheryl has a bruise on her chin that could have been from Kent's fist."

"I'm sure Cheryl isn't the only one in town who has bruises," the judge commented.

"Yes, but she's a volunteer firefighter," I countered. "She knows how to start a fire. Plus, I found that badge at the scene. It was a Foxdancer Lodge badge. It could have been hers."

"Or any of the dozen people working here," he said. "Any one of which could have had a perfectly innocent reason to be visiting Kent Banner and have dropped their badge. You heard The Badge Guy the day we got here. Those lanyards have safety clasps on them. They come apart without a lot of tugging."

"I think Luke Shipley might also be on the suspect list. The badge might be his, and I'll admit he came up to me this afternoon in the café and expressed concern that he might be a suspect."

"That's two likely suspects, but there could be more." The judge held up his hands. "Cheryl. Luke. The pot guy Rocky threw under the bus. Heck, maybe *Rocky* wanted the guy dead. Or The Badge Guy. Or Peabody Mann. Or the cashier at the donut shop."

"Not the donut shop cashier!" I protested with a laugh. "You're right; it could be anyone. But it's still kind of fun to play sleuth while on vacation."

We sat for a few seconds while I thought once more about my conversation with Cheryl and her bruise.

"What do you know about head wounds?" I mused, half to myself.

"I know that even minor ones bleed like you're dying. I had a ceiling lamp fall on my head while I was changing the bulb once. I didn't even need stitches, but the bedroom looked like a crime scene." Judge Beck rubbed his head at the memory. "Is that what killed him? I thought the rumor mill said smoke inhalation?"

"Until the coroner weighs in, it *is* all rumors. We don't know if the head wound was a factor or not. Heck, for all I know the guy had a lamp fall on his head that morning and it had nothing to do with his death."

The judge nodded. "Or he was trying to put out the fire and got conked on the head by a falling beam in the barn."

It was a solid possibility. "So, the guy had a head wound, but maybe it wasn't that bad," I conjectured. "Maybe it bled a lot and knocked him out for a minute or so, he got up, and he went into the barn and died of smoke inhalation trying to put out the fire. Or like you said, a falling beam killed him."

"And the fire he was trying to put out started because he took a candle into the barn and accidently knocked it over?" The judge raised an eyebrow.

I rolled my eyes. "No, of course not. And despite what Peabody is going to write in his next book, I doubt the fire marshal would have ruled the fire an arson if it had started from a candle. Maybelle said it was gasoline splashed on the walls. I can't imagine Kent Banner just happened to have dropped a lit candle in five gallons of spilled gas."

"True." The judge sighed. "Drawing from my experience in hearing these sorts of cases, I'm going to say the arsonist is most likely the murderer. Yes, there's a possibility they were separate actions, or that the death was an accidental effect of the arson, but the likelier scenario is that one person did both intentionally."

I over at him. "You've had an arson with a homicide in your court before?"

He nodded. "And I've read more cases than you can count where someone tried to cover up a murder with arson. It's typically the same story—the murder wasn't planned, or wasn't well planned, and the killer thinks the fire is going to destroy any evidence that might lead to him or her. News-flash—it doesn't."

I pursed my lips. "At least in the cases brought before the court, it didn't. If the fire did destroy the evidence, then you'd never know, right? Those cases would just be ruled as accidental, fire-related deaths, and no one besides the killer and the victim would be the wiser."

"True." He took a quick sip of his wine. "But I'm willing to bet in the majority of cases, the killer is caught."

"Optimist," I teased.

"Pessimist," he shot back.

"I prefer to call myself a realist."

It was his turn to roll his eyes. "Fine, realist then. So, who are your other suspects besides our own Julie McCoy and the young blond Adonis of a ski instructor that my daughter is infatuated with?"

"Well, there *is* the pothead. Rocky says the local marijuana grower might have killed the guy over a drug territory dispute, but I don't see that."

"Yeah, I'm not even going to count that one." The judge shook his head. "In my experience, which is limited to the courtroom, dealers who push the hard stuff don't really care about people selling weed and vice-versa."

"Limited to the courtroom?" I smothered a laugh. "Don't tell me you never smoked pot when you were young."

He raised a hand. "Never."

"Not even a toke off a friend's joint?"

"Nope. I had career aspirations even in my youth and knew that that sort of thing could ruin my chances." He shot me a sideways look. "By your easy use of the jargon, I'm assuming you did indeed toke your friend's joint?"

I grinned. "I'm not going to tell you since you're such an upstanding citizen and upholder of the law. I will admit I didn't smoke at all after college."

He nodded. "I'm glad I don't have to haul you into rehab or anything. So, we're crossing the local marijuana grower off our list. Who's next?"

"Like you said earlier, pretty much everyone in town. So many residents seem to have a deep commitment to keeping the town's reputation clean. The only crimes they'll admit to are the quirky ones that add local flavor. I'll go ahead and add Rocky as well as that cashier at the donut shop," I teased. "Heck, even Peabody. He's already rewriting history from twenty-four hours ago to suit the town's narrative. But right now, my money is on Cheryl."

"Mine too," he agreed.

"There could be all sorts of people with means, motive, and opportunity," I continued. "Maybe the man *was* involved in drug distribution, was skimming off the top, and his bosses took care of the problem. Maybe he ran out on debts to a loan shark, and they tracked him down. Maybe the new owner wanted to burn the place down for insurance reasons, and the tenant caught him, so he killed the tenant."

"So, we just leave it in the hands of the detective, then." Judge Beck's lips twitched.

"While the official investigation is indeed in the hands of the detective, I'm far too curious not to be poking my nose into the case." I sighed, thinking that we'd be leaving in another three days, and murder investigations didn't always move along that quickly. Maybe I could subscribe to an electronic copy of the local paper so I could follow from back home. Or just call Maybelle and Evie every few days for an update.

"Well, I'm curious too. Let me know what your snooping reveals." Judge Beck reached forward and handed me my wine. "And drink up. The kids will be back soon, and I plan on being in bed right after they arrive."

I yawned and sipped my wine. "Me too."

CHAPTER 9

I desperately wanted to sleep in, but Madison and Henry were up with the sun, ordering room service breakfast and racing around in preparation for another day on the slopes.

"Aren't you tired?" I asked Madison as I struggled to pull on a pair of leggings. My leg muscles were tight. My arm muscles were tight. My butt muscles were tight. I was pretty sure even my finger and toe muscles were tight.

"Nope. I can't wait to get out there again. I met a couple of girls last night, and we agreed to ski together after my lesson. The guy running the quad lift today is super cute, according to Sierra."

"Well, I'll have to check him out myself," I told her. "I'll taking the quad lift today as well."

Tackling moguls, if I could manage to work up my nerve. I wasn't happy about that, but if I didn't face my fears, I'd regret it. There probably wouldn't be a lot of opportunities for me to spend a week out west skiing with private lessons every day. If I wanted to improve, now was the time to do it.

Besides, I wasn't getting any younger. Better to roll down a mogul field at sixty than do it at eighty.

I was the last one into the common room, but it seemed that the kids had ordered enough food for a small army. There were omelets, pancakes, French toast, a bowl of mixed berries, yogurt, and a tray of bacon. I made a beeline to the most important thing on the table this morning—the coffee. The judge beat me there and poured us both a mug.

"How are you feeling this morning?" he asked as he handed me my coffee.

"Tired. Stiff. I'm not used to this level of physical activity for hours at a stretch." I sipped from my mug, feeling better already. "Once I'm moving, I'll be okay, but I don't think I'm going to be on the slopes much past my lesson."

"Take the SUV back to the lodge if you want," he urged. "I'll leave you the keys and call you when we're ready to go. Honestly, I might come back early myself."

I shrugged. "Don't on my account. I can go shopping, or read, or relax in the hot tub, or even take a nap. It's not like I'll be bored."

"Okay. Let's plan on Madison, Henry, and I coming back at three. That'll give us time to shower, change, and unwind before dinner. The kids will probably do the slopes here after eating, and us old folks can put our feet up and relax."

"Or get a massage," Madison chimed in. "Red says there's a spa in town."

Maybe I'd swing over after lunch. I might need a massage after my mogul field attempt today. Or possibly a trip to the emergency room.

Judge Beck glanced at his watch. "Eat up. We need to get going in fifteen."

Henry grabbed a piece of bacon and shoved it in his mouth. I quickly ate half an omelet and a bowl of fruit, pouring some coffee into a go-cup for the drive over.

At the resort, we stored our stuff in the locker, the judge putting the car keys in mine so I could head back early if I wanted. Outside, we snapped on our skis and boards and made our way over to where the instructors were to meet us. Even though Judge Beck wasn't taking daily lessons, he continued to wait with us each morning. Skittles, Henry's instructor, came to get him first. I saw Madison's smile falter as Red boarded up to her. She quickly hid her disappointment and headed off with the young man.

"Luke isn't here again today?" the judge murmured.

What had the young man missing two days of work in a row? He'd been upset yesterday, saying he knew he'd be a suspect in the murder and arson. Hopefully, the reason for his absence was that he'd gone to consult with an attorney.

It wasn't just Luke's absence on my mind, though. I was dying to know what the detective had discovered about the badge I'd found. Had it been Luke's? Cheryl's? Did the person have a convincing reason why their badge had been found at a crime scene? I was sure Detective Burnside was busy figuring that all out, and I really wanted to be a fly on the wall of his office right now.

I'm pretty sure Maybelle *was* a fly on the wall of his office or at least as near a one as she could be. If anyone knew what was going on, it was her. I didn't have her number, but I did have Evie's and had completely forgotten to return her call from last night. If I didn't hear anything by the time I was done with my lesson, I was going to call her and find out what she knew.

Gus skied up, I waved Judge Beck goodbye for the morning, and with a churning feeling in my stomach, the instructor and I headed to the huge lift that went all the way up and would allow us access to the more difficult slopes.

"So, what did you decide?" Gus asked as we settled into the lift chair.

I took a deep breath and slowly let it out. "Moguls. But if I die, I'm haunting you. Poltergeist haunting. Stuff flying off shelves, banging noises in the middle of the night. That's the kind of haunting I'm talking about."

"You'll be fine, Kay," Gus reassured me. "You're a good skier. Cautious. Sensible. Always thinking ahead. Just remember the techniques we worked on yesterday, follow my lead, and you'll do fine."

I nodded, desperately needing to change the subject to something that didn't threaten to send me into a panic attack.

"We went to downtown Crow Creek last night and heard Peabody Mann speak at the library," I told him.

"He really packs them in each week." Gus's tone was even and cautious—which told me a lot about how he viewed Peabody. "The guy makes a fortune in book sales. His garage is filled with boxes of them, and I'm pretty sure he sells out every year."

"Since you have to run the gauntlet past his table and sales pitch to get out of the library, I can imagine. The judge and I each bought one of his books," I confessed.

Gus chuckled. "Suckers."

"It seemed terribly rude to leave a free, and very entertaining, mind you, presentation and *not* buy one of his books. I think Judge Beck is going to keep his, probably stick it on the shelf in the parlor and forget he ever bought it. I'll give mine to my friend Daisy. She loves old-time scandalous stories like that."

"Daisy is your morning yoga partner?"

I was impressed with his memory of my nervous rambling conversation the other day. "My best friend. Yoga with her every morning got me through a lot of tough times. It's less about exercise and more about emotional therapy."

"Yoga often is," Gus mused.

"So, you're not a fan of the local historian?" I asked, turning the conversation back to the talk at the library.

"Historian isn't the word I'd use. Peabody does more than embellish sometimes. I'll admit it's great for tourism, and the guy makes bank off his schtick, but too many of the locals are willing to ignore the fact that Crow Creek has it's dark elements just like any other town and believe the very sanitized version Peabody peddles."

"He told me the spin he was going to put on the fire at the old Shipley farm." I sniffed and shook my head. "In his mind, the tenant went out to the barn with a candle, of all things, and fell asleep. His death was a tragic accident and so was the fire."

Gus snorted. "He's going to have a hard time selling that one since they arrested Luke Shipley this morning."

"What!" I jerked around, grateful for the safety bar since my motion sent the chair swinging. "They arrested Luke Shipley? On what charges?"

"Assault and murder—at least that's what I hear around the coffee shop this morning. Rumor mill said the prosecutor is pushing second degree but will probably take a manslaughter plea." He shook his head. "I've lived here long enough to know better. The town will want this to go away, so it will all end up being self-defense with probation and community service. The Shipleys are an old family in Crow Creek, and the town takes care of its own."

I shivered a little at his last statement, thinking of Peabody's revisionist history, of Rocky and Cheryl's insistence that Crow Creek was the perfect town. Gus was probably right. I shouldn't worry about Luke. But I did.

"That would be one case where I'd agree with a slap on the wrist."

He eyed me in surprise. "You're a private investigator. You're living with a judge. You seriously don't think he should serve time? I mean, from what I heard in town, he went out there and got into a fight with the guy, then knocked him upside the head with some sort of farming implement and set a fire to cover it up."

It didn't seem possible. Luke. He'd been trying to buy the place, to get his family farm back. "Why would he get into a fight with Kent Banner?"

Gus lifted a shoulder. "Banner was buying the farm."

"But Bajaj wasn't going to sell," I sputtered. "Luke had made him an offer, and he didn't want to sell the property. Why would he refuse to sell it to Luke, then turn around and sell it to a tenant?"

Especially a tenant no one liked, one that everyone believed was conducting illegal activities on the farm.

Gus held up his hands. "Maybe Banner offered him more? Maybe he didn't want to sell, but Banner is a buddy of his, so he changed his mind?"

Maybe Banner was blackmailing him. That's where my suspicious mind immediately went. I'd clearly been hanging around Evie and Maybelle too long.

"I guess." I sighed, my heart heavy about Luke. Had it really been him? He'd been so earnest yesterday about his innocence. He'd wanted to hire me. What if he *was* innocent?

"How did they discover it was Luke?" I asked, wanting to know the evidence.

"I heard that they found his badge at the barn."

I shook my head. "There has to be more than that. Detective Burnside seems like a good investigator. I can't believe he'd arrest someone just over a badge that could have been dropped any time over the last few months."

I hated that I'd been the one to find it, to turn it in. The ghost had pointed it out to me, flicked it over to me in a poltergeist action. Maybelle had been asking the spirit to reveal who had been the murderer, and he'd led me to the badge. Was the ghost lying? Or maybe Luke really *had* killed the man.

Even if it had been an accident, setting the fire to cover it up was going to make the death look premeditated. Poor Luke.

"Kent Banner shot at Cheryl," I threw out there. "And she shot back at him. They had some sort of feud going on. Clearly, she should be a suspect as well. And the DEA was looking into the man for drug trafficking. Rocky thinks maybe Silas was involved because of their competing interests."

Okay, now I was just throwing out names in the desperate hope that the killer really wasn't Luke Shipley.

"*Silas*? The guy who grows pot in his basement and out back behind his garage?" Gus grinned. "You've got to be kidding me. Rocky needs to have his head examined if he thinks Silas would kill anyone."

I sighed. "Maybe Luke did it. If so, I do think he should pay for his crime, but I hate seeing a young person's life ruined. The guy shot at Cheryl. What if Luke went out there to talk to him, and Kent Banner started shooting at him too? What if he did act in self-defense?"

I thought of Peony and how a selfish, careless blackmail attempt had landed her with a murder conviction and a year in juvie. I thought of Melvin Elmer, how he'd gotten away with murder, and how I'd struggled with conflicting thoughts of what justice really was. Judge Beck had it easy. He looked to the law, and any moral ambiguity that resulted from its application was deflected to the legislature and the appeals courts. Did he rest easy at night, relying on prior case law and judgments to do the right thing? Or did he toss and turn in his bed as I had, wishing things had gone differently?

"I honestly don't think Kent Banner was doing drug distribution," Gus added. "I do a lot of backcountry skiing in that area, and I never saw anyone coming and going from his driveway except for the UPS guy."

I choked back a laugh at the thought of someone using UPS to ship drugs.

"Seriously. It seemed like every afternoon around four, the big brown truck would drive up to the old Shipley house."

"Maybe he buys a lot of stuff off the internet," I agreed. "It doesn't mean he isn't involved in something illegal. I'm pretty sure even criminals shop online."

Gus nodded. "I don't buy the whole drug cartel thing. Peabody makes up stories to sanitize everything, but we've got others in town who do the opposite. Strangers and newcomers moving into the area get some pretty intense scrutiny. When Phil Bancock first moved here eight years ago, everyone was convinced he was in the witness protection program and that at any moment a bunch of mafia hitmen were going to descend on the town to take revenge on him for snitching. And when I moved here ten years ago, rumors were flying that I was a bigamist with three wives."

I blinked at him. "How did anyone come up with that?"

He shrugged. "Who knows? I've been married twice, but not at the same time, and my sister helped me move in and get settled. I guess me being a bigamist was more interesting than a divorced guy switching careers and moving out of the city."

"So, you weren't always a ski instructor?"

"I've always been a ski instructor, but the last decade I've done it part time during the season, mainly for the free lift passes. Full time I was project manager."

I nodded. "In IT?"

He laughed. "In construction. Don't get me wrong, I like computers as much as anyone, but I'd rather spend my days organizing construction crews. Or with a hammer in my hand."

"Or a set of skis on your feet?" I grinned.

"Absolutely."

I looked down at the skiers so far below as they headed down the slopes and felt a pang of sympathy for Luke Shipley.

"Who do you think might have had a problem with Kent Banner, aside from Luke? Assuming the drug story is just a wild tale, that is." I turned back to Gus.

"Besides Cheryl?" He held up his hands. "Heck if I know. The guy's not a complete hermit, but he doesn't socialize around town that I'm aware of. He clearly gets a lot of UPS shipments. Other than that, the only vehicle I've ever seen out there when I'm skiing is the lodge truck."

I instantly thought of the red truck with the discreet logo on the side. "The lodge truck? As in Foxdancer Lodge?"

Gus nodded. "The back trail sweeps past the old Shipley property. I know at one point Rocky wanted to use a section where there's some cross-country skiing trails for his customers."

Rocky had mentioned that, and that I'd assumed the trail that the judge and I had inadvertently ended up on had been the one he'd wanted to use.

"He told us that was a done deal," I said. "Rocky claimed the new trail would be open in a few weeks."

Gus snorted. "Any guy who shoots at Cheryl cutting across his property isn't going to want skiers practically in his back yard. There's no way Rocky was getting access to that land unless the owner okayed it."

The lodge truck had been out there. Gus had seen it before. And I was more convinced than ever that was the truck I'd seen going down the road the night of the fire.

"I can't imagine the owner okaying it," I commented.

"Unless he was selling Banner the farm and Rocky the land where the trail is."

Gus shook his head. "Rocky is outgoing and friendly, but he's cheap, sneaky, and self-serving. I doubt he'd buy the land or even compensate the owner for its use. I'm guessing Rocky went up there to talk to Kent Banner to see if he could do a workaround where the owner never found out he was using the trails."

Did Kent Banner shoot at Rocky as well? Did they argue? What happened when Rocky didn't get what he wanted? But what would Rocky gain with Kent Banner's death?

Unless…with Kent dead, maybe Luke would buy the farm and *he'd* be more willing to cut a deal with Rocky?

"You don't like Rocky?" Judging from Gus's tone, Peabody wasn't the only person in Crow Creek he disapproved of.

"The guy's not bad. I just think he's a little used-car, if you get my meaning." Gus wrinkled his nose. "He can put whatever spin he wants on the lodge and the town, but that doesn't mean the rest of us need to go along with it. We're normal people. I'm not going to agree to dance to his crazy-town music."

"If the tenant said no to Rocky, maybe he's the one who killed him and started the fire," I voiced my earlier thoughts. "Then there would be no one to block him from using the trails."

Gus laughed. "Now *that* belongs in a book."

We slid off the chair lift, skied to the top of the hill, then stopped. I looked over the edge, my stomach churning at the field of snow-covered bumps.

"We're going to do this in a rhythm, just like you were doing the last two days, but instead of fast-slow, we're going to count, plant our pole, then turn. Keep your weight on the downhill ski."

I nodded. "Are we turning on the side of the mogul or on the top?"

"Turning is easier on the top. Skiing in between the bumps means you have to go faster and you'll have less time to make decisions about the next mogul."

My hands were already sweating.

"Flexible ankles, knees, and hips. Think of your legs as springs. We're going to pick a spot to aim for past the mogul field and keep our attention focused on getting there."

I jabbed a pole into the snow, already frustrated. "I can't focus on the bottom of the hill *and* focus on navigating the moguls."

"Follow me." His voice was calm and confident. "See how the mogul field is only on part of the slope? We're just going to do four or five bumps, then pull out of the field and evaluate what's next. Maybe we do more; maybe we just ski down the hill. This first trip down all I want you to do is keep your legs flexible and follow my lead."

"And not run you over," I muttered.

He laughed. "Ideally, yeah. That's my problem to worry about though, not yours."

I nodded, took a few deep breaths, then lowered my goggles. "Ready when you are."

I was so not ready. As we hovered at the edge of the slope, I found myself wishing I'd brought a flask and taken a few swigs of liquid courage before attempting this. Before I had time to do more than think about it, we were off. I kept Gus in view, following his path and banking off the sides of the moguls. Instead of four or five, we did eight, then Gus led me out of the bumps and off to the side where we slid to a stop.

"How was that?" he asked.

I still felt like I was going to throw up, but I'd done it. No broken bones. No falling and ending up stuck between the mounds of snow.

"Not terrible," I admitted. "In the past I'd go all the way to the top of the mogul hill to turn and sometimes end up overshooting and jumping them—then crashing. Because of that, I think I overcompensated and stayed too far down in the trench. I was too afraid to go fast, so I'd end up panicking, trying to slow down, and then crashing in the trench."

"Go halfway to three quarters of the way up the side and use the bumps to turn," Gus told me. "Like we just did. When you get more comfortable, you can go up higher or increase speed and stay in the valley between the moguls, navigating around them."

I laughed. "I'll be happy just to get down in one piece."

He motioned with one of his poles. "Then you're going to be happy. We're going back in and do some more, then out like we just did. We'll take this little bits at a time until you feel comfortable. Or we can quit now, and you can say you gave it a shot and didn't like it."

I couldn't say I actually liked it, but I'd come this far and wasn't about to give up. "Let's keep doing the little bits like you suggested, then I'll decide when we're down the mountain if I want to do it again."

He grinned at me. "Deal."

By the time we were on flat snow, I'd made up my mind. Moguls weren't horrible. I wasn't ready for anything advanced, but I was pretty sure I could face a small mogul field without losing my breakfast. Gus and I continued to go down the same slope, taking the bumps in little chunks until the end of my lesson.

I hadn't fallen. I hadn't embarrassed myself. I hadn't broken any bones. And I was willing to admit that I was having fun. Thank goodness I'd faced my fears, trusted my instructor to not push me beyond my capabilities, and given it a try.

Moguls. I could check that off my list. And I might actually go down that slope a few more times without Gus, now that I knew what I was doing.

I said my goodbyes to Gus and skied straight to one of the outdoor tables of the café. There was this feeling of smug satisfaction in my chest along with the shaky anxiety that had come in the wake of all that adrenaline. I'd done it. I'd managed to make it through a mogul field without getting stuck between two mounds of snow on my butt and having to yank my skis off to walk out.

I'd made it through. And best of all, Gus had taught me how to get myself going again if I ever found myself on my rear wedged between the mounds of snow. I could manage moguls, and maybe by the end of the week I'd even appear somewhat confident while doing skiing them.

Skis off and a mug of coffee with an indulgent heaping of whipped cream in hand, I checked my phone.

Cheryl had left a message that the lodge van was available tonight if the judge and I wanted to reserve it.

Evie had called again to tell me that Luke Shipley had been arrested and to give a miffed condemnation of Kent Banner's ghost, who didn't even have the courtesy of clueing her and Maybelle in about the murderer.

The last message was from Luke Shipley. He assured me right away that he had a lawyer but wanted to see me. His bail hearing was this afternoon, and he hoped I could pick him up at the county jail so we could talk. If not, he said he'd try to reach me at the lodge later.

I glanced at the time, then pulled up a map to the Pitkin County Jail on my phone's GPS, just to see where it was. Oddly, it was six blocks from the main resort. I could have walked there, although I had no intention of doing that, especially in snow boots.

I changed shoes, then drove the SUV down to the jail. An hour later, Luke Shipley had climbed into the passenger side of the vehicle, and we were on our way back to Crow Creek. The judge would probably have a fit that I was giving someone who'd been arrested on murder charges a lift home, but I wasn't afraid of Luke.

"They ended up charging me with assault, not murder," he quickly reassured me as he fastened his seatbelt. "I'm sure the murder charges are coming, but my lawyer said they'd need to wait for the coroner's official report first."

I resisted the urge to pat his shoulder. "So, the badge at the scene was yours?" I asked him, trying to figure out the evidence.

"They say it is." Luke made a frustrated noise. "It's not, though. I've got my badge. I didn't lose it. I haven't lost a badge in over a year."

I frowned. "Could it have been that badge from a year ago? Maybe you went out to your family farm last year sometime and it snapped off and has been there ever since?"

He shook his head. "I'll admit I've gone by occasionally to check things out, but I'm pretty sure I lost that badge last year on the lodge slopes somewhere. And it's not *that* badge. My lawyer told me the badge they found was the one that was issued last year, that it was my current badge. But it's not. I've got that one." He dug around in a plastic bag that held his belongings from the jail. "Here. See?"

I was intrigued enough to pull over and look at the badge. "Do you mind if I snap a few pictures of this?"

He shrugged. "Go ahead."

Not only did I take a picture, but I also jotted down the number above the bar code in my phone. Then I flipped the badge over and saw a sticker on the back of it—an adorable little pika with rounded ears and dark eyes.

Suddenly I remembered that first day we'd arrived, remembered Madison talking with Luke as he helped her with her fitting. I remembered Madison holding his badge as she flirted with him. She'd taken the last pika sticker from the shop. I could absolutely see her attaching the sticker to his badge. It was such a teenage girl thing to do, and Luke did not strike me as the kind of young man that would choose a cute rabbit-like animal to decorate the back of his badge.

"Madison put that on there." He looked embarrassed. "The glue is insane on those stickers. They're impossible to get off, and I'm not paying ten bucks to replace a badge because of a pika sticker."

"They're impossible to get off," I mused. Flipping the badge back over, I looked at the front with the lodge logo and two somewhat worn stickers from the major resorts where he taught.

He needed those stickers for the lifts. The badge the ghost had tossed at me hadn't had those stickers. There was no way Luke could have had a badge for a year and *not* have lift stickers for the other resorts on it.

And the sticker on the back was proof that he hadn't lost his badge the night of the fire. Madison would testify that she'd put the sticker on the back the day before the fire, when Kent Banner was supposedly alive and well.

The badge I'd found...had it been planted? If so, the culprit would have needed access to the badge making system and the computer in order to print one out and assign it to Luke—and to back date it a year.

But a badge shouldn't have been enough to have him brought up on assault charges, let alone murder.

"So, tell me what happened," I said as I pulled back out onto the road.

"I was there," he blurted out. "I got an e-mail from Mr. Bajaj saying that he was going to sell the farm to Kent Banner instead of me. I...I don't have any more money. I offered the maximum of what the bank would loan me. I was going to lose my home once more, after living like a pauper and saving for two years."

This time I did reach out and pat his shoulder.

"Anyway, I went out there to talk to Banner. Everyone says he's a jerk, but I'd never met him. I figured if I could talk to him and tell him my story that maybe he'd back out of the purchase. There are other farms he could buy. I hoped to beg him not to buy mine."

"Oh, Luke." My heart broke for the guy. After Eli had died, I'd been faced with the decision of selling our home or heading for foreclosure. The old Victorian hadn't been in my family for generations, but it had become home to me, and it would have hurt to see it go. I could only imagine how much worse it had been for Luke.

"It was before sunset when I got out there—maybe around four? Banner hadn't come out of the house when I parked, and…I looked around." He glanced over at me sheepishly. "I know I was trespassing at that point, but it hurt to see the house like that, so neglected, and I went around to the barn and the stables. Part of it was nostalgia, part of it was frustration. How could this place be worth more than I'd offered? It was falling down. Surely I was the only one who'd want to pay over the market value for it."

"What did you see in the stables? In the barn?" The memory of those melted plastic tables popped into my mind.

"I just took a quick peek in the barn. He had about six of those plastic tables set up and a bunch of leaves and stuff were spread out on them."

I blinked at that. Leaves? Not bricks of heroin? Was Kent Banner doing something with marijuana and not illegal controlled substances? Was Rocky right, and some competition existed between Kent and Silas?

"There was nothing in the stables besides the usual stuff—

some old tack that was covered in mold, grooming and farrier supplies, pitchforks and shovels."

I nodded, still wondering what the heck had been on those tables. Had it all burned up in the fire? Had Kent Banner removed it all *before* the fire?

"I heard someone yell, and a gunshot, and nearly wet my pants." Luke let out a slow breath. "I turned around and Banner was right behind me, yelling and pointing a shotgun at me. I figured any appeal I'd been about to make was going to fall on deaf ears, but I tried anyway. He wanted to know what I was doing snooping around his place, and I told him who I was and that I wanted to buy the farm back. He wasn't even paying attention. He kept coming closer, with that gun pointed at me, yelling about trespassers."

Good grief, it was a wonder Luke hadn't gotten himself killed. "What happened?"

"I backed up, but the stable was behind me, and there was nowhere I could go. I wasn't about to turn my back on him and run. He shot at Cheryl. He'd just shot what I assumed was a warning, but for all I knew, he was going to kill me." Luke fidgeted in his seat. "I reached down, grabbed an old hoof stand that was next to one of the stall doors, and I hit him with it."

"A hoof stand?" For some reason I was envisioning a platform, like a stage, but Luke wouldn't have been able to heft something like that up in the air.

"It's a tool. Farriers use them for trimming horse hoofs. New ones are lightweight plastic, but this was an old one, so it was kind of heavy." He winced when he said that.

My heart sank. "Was he okay when you left?"

"I don't know." His laugh was bitter. "He staggered to the side and fell. I panicked and ran, thinking I needed to get the heck out of there before he shot me. I honestly don't know if

I hit him hard enough to kill him or not. I'm definitely guilty of assault—and maybe of murder."

"You're guilty of trespass and self-defense," I told him. "And hopefully your lawyer is going to use that in your trial. Just because you were snooping around doesn't give anyone the right to shoot at you and threaten you with a rifle!"

"In some states it does." His tone was matter of fact. "I don't know if I killed him or not, but the police report said Banner had a visible wound to his head when they found his body."

"But rumors are the coroner's report is going to say he died of smoke inhalation, not the head wound," I reassured him.

"Maybe. Maybe not. For all I know, he lost consciousness, and that's why he died in the fire. If that's the case, then his death is still my fault."

"But you didn't set the fire," I countered. "And it wasn't a random accident. If Kent Banner was drying pot or whatever out in that barn, he hardly would have been dumping gasoline all over the place and lighting candles. Someone deliberately set that fire, and it's that person who is guilty of murder, not you."

He took a deep breath and let it out with a whoosh. "I hope you're right, Ms. Carrera."

I hoped so, too. "You hit him right outside the stables?" I asked, wondering if that was close to where the badge had been found. "Where exactly was he when you ran?"

"Yes, we were outside the barn, around back where the stables were. The hoof stand was propped up against one of the stall doors. When I hit him, he fell to the side, partially into one of the stalls." He frowned in thought. "The third from the end, I think. The door was missing off that one."

Hadn't someone said the body was found inside the barn, not out back by the stables? If Kent Banner had died of smoke inhalation, then he *had* to have been inside the barn. That meant the man hadn't been injured so badly that he couldn't get up and go inside or go into the barn to check if Luke had tampered with anything.

And then there was the timing. Luke was there around four in the evening. Sunset was at five-forty-five, give or take a few minutes. We'd been in the dining room at four and on the slopes by five, which meant it was probably closer to five thirty or even sunset when the judge and I had seen the faint curl of smoke. The fire had most likely been started not long before we'd arrived—which would have been at least a half an hour after Luke had left. That *had* to give Luke some sort of alibi.

"Where did you go afterward?" I asked him.

"Home." He picked at the bag holding his belongings. "I live on the other side of Crow Creek. I got home, went inside, and made dinner. No one saw me that I'm aware of."

I frowned, thinking of something else. "Where exactly did you park when you went to see Kent Banner?"

There had been another set of tracks next to Banner's car, but I hadn't seen a third set when the judge and I had skied up to the house.

"Around the side of the barn. That's probably why Banner didn't see me when I first arrived. I always parked beside the barn when I lived there."

We hadn't gone close enough to the barn to see any tracks, since it had been on fire when we'd arrived. If those tracks beside Kent Banner's car hadn't been Luke's, then whose were they? Probably the same person who'd most likely driven out the next day and dumped a faked badge for the police—or me—to find.

I pulled up to the address he'd given me. Luke was living in a big block, three-story building with a sign outside that proclaimed one bedroom and efficiency apartments were available now.

"Tell your lawyer," I said as he made to get out of the SUV. "Call him as soon as you're inside and tell him everything you just told me about the badge, the stuff on the tables in the barn, and where Kent Banner fell when you hit him."

He nodded, thanked me for the ride and the advice, then headed into the apartments. I watched him until he was inside, debating where I wanted to head next. The lodge? Or out to the old Shipley farm?

CHAPTER 10

J went ahead and hauled my skis and equipment to the room after parking the SUV in the lodge's lot, then went back downstairs. The lobby was quiet, all the guests either on the slopes or off doing some other activity. There was a young woman in the gift shop behind the counter who I'd never seen before. She looked up from her cell phone, guiltily stashing it under the counter as she smiled at me.

"Is...The Badge Guy in?" I felt like a total idiot for not ever finding out his name.

Her brow wrinkled for a second, then cleared. "Eric? He'll be in tomorrow morning. Are you having a problem with yours? I can call Cheryl, or see if Rocky is in."

"No, that's okay."

As far as I knew, The Badge Guy, Eric, wasn't a suspect, but Cheryl definitely was in my book, and possibly Rocky. The woman eyed me as I thought through which of my questions she might be able to answer.

Much to her obvious dismay, I didn't leave.

"Are they the only three who have access to the badge system?"

She nodded. "Yeah. Rocky locked it down a few years back after he caught one of the desk clerks printing all access badges for her friends. Are you sure you don't want me to call one of them?"

"No need. Can the badge data be altered in any way?" I asked. "Like change a limited access to all access? Change the effective dates of the badge? Can that be done, or would a new badge need to be made up?"

She shrugged, gaze drifting to the spot under the counter where she'd stashed her phone. "I don't know. I could call Cheryl? Or Rocky?"

"No," I repeated. Clearly, I'd exhausted the extent of this employee's knowledge. "One last thing. Can I grab one of the animal stickers to decorate the back of my badge?"

That earned me an exasperated look, but she pulled the tray up and set it on the counter.

"Are there any more pika stickers?" I asked, pointing at the empty section.

"They're all gone. Eric ordered more, but they probably won't be in for a few more days." She pulled out a black bear and held it out to me. "How about this one? He's super cute."

I took it and stuck it on the back of my badge beside the bighorn sheep sticker. "Thanks."

The cashier went back to her cell phone, visibly relieved as I made my way out of the gift shop.

Eric wouldn't be in until tomorrow. I gritted my teeth in frustration but didn't want to tip my hand and start asking Cheryl or Rocky. That left one thing for me to check out, and luckily, I had a few more hours until I needed to pick the judge and the kids up at the resort.

As I pulled down the drive to the old Shipley farm, I saw two patrol cars and a sedan parked beside Kent Banner's vehicle. I should have turned around and left, but I'm nosy, so I parked next to the sedan and walked up to the house.

Detective Burnside was standing on the front porch next to the open door. I could see four uniformed officers inside the house. He waved a handful of papers at me as I climbed to the porch.

"Warrant." His grin was triumphant.

"What are you hoping to find?" I eyed the stack of paper.

"Correspondence, cell phone records. That sort of thing."

"Drugs." I smirked. "Can I admit that I saw baggies, boxes, and a scale in the kitchen? Plus a dehydrator? And someone else saw leafy stuff spread out on the plastic tables in the barn, presumably for drying."

"If there are any drugs or clear drug paraphernalia in clear view, we'll grab it." The guy was obviously dying to share but keeping quiet because of the case being open.

"Well, if you see a pen on the floor in the kitchen, to the left of the door, can you grab it? I dropped it trying to move the curtain aside through a hole in the window."

He rolled his eyes and didn't reply. I doubted I'd ever get that pen back, darn it.

"I don't know if Luke's attorney has contacted you yet, but that badge isn't his," I commented, shifting my thoughts from the lost pen back to the mystery at hand.

The detective's brows lifted at that.

I went on. "I didn't realize it until today, but there were no lift stickers on the front of the badge. You can't tell me that Luke worked for a year getting on and off the lifts at the various resorts in and around Aspen without any lift stickers."

"Maybe they know him," he countered.

"All of them? For a year? At two huge resorts?"

"That's a valid point," he said with a nod.

I continued. "That's not all. The day we arrived, the day of the fire, my friend's daughter put a pika sticker on the back of Luke Shipley's badge. It's still there on the one he's carrying around with him. Why would he have a second badge? And if so, why would he have switched his badges out before going to see Kent Banner, then dropped the secondary one knowing it would be traced back to him? None of that makes sense. It's not his badge. Someone's trying to frame him. *That's* what makes sense."

"He could have gotten a replacement one later that night and put one of those pica stickers on it, trying to make it look like the original badge." The detective shrugged, looking as if he didn't quite believe that himself.

"But the one I found didn't have a sticker, and that glue is like cement." I turned my own badge over and tried in vain to get the bear sticker off the back, only succeeding in fraying it a bit around the edges. "See? Besides, there aren't any more pika stickers. Madison took the last one, and they won't have any more in for another few days. I just confirmed with the gift shop. So unless you think Luke has been hoarding stickers, just in case he loses his badge and needs an alibi, this gets him off the hook."

"No, it doesn't get him off the hook," the detective corrected. "He admitted to assaulting Kent Banner. That blow might have been the one to kill him. Maybe there's someone else involved who is trying to pin it *all* on Luke, but either way, the boy is facing some trouble."

"But he's not facing arson charges," I argued. "Check the timing of when Luke says he was here and when the judge called in the fire. It doesn't add up. Plus, just before we skied over to the farm and saw the fire, I saw a truck driving down the road. A red truck with something on the side. I think it was a lodge truck."

"Cheryl does live down this road, and she works at the lodge," he reminded me.

"She claims no one but Rocky drives that truck. And even if it was her, why didn't she notice the fire and call it in? How could she, a volunteer firefighter, drive right past a barn with smoke coming out of it and not at least stop to investigate?"

The detective waved the comments off. "She might not have seen it from the road or been distracted and not looking at the farm. It might have been some other truck, not the one from the lodge. Right now, I've got a piece of evidence that puts Luke Shipley at the scene, and his confession that he hit Kent Banner upside the head. Assault. And maybe murder. It's still an open investigation, Ms. Carrera. We charged the boy with assault, but I'm not ready to move forward with anything else until I'm done turning all the stones over. And if what's under those stones continues to point at Luke Shipley, then we'll add charges. If not...then we'll head down that other road and see where it takes us."

That should have been a comfort, but it wasn't. Detective Burnside hadn't given me any reason to doubt his investigative abilities but thinking about the mess that young man had gotten himself into, thinking about him possibly having to serve jail time, upset me.

"Surely the fact that someone tried to set him up tells you there's a much worse person out there than Luke Shipley. He was just defending himself," I insisted. "And he didn't start that fire."

Detective Burnside sighed. "Luke's a good kid. Family's been around here forever. Most of the town was rooting for him to buy this place back. I don't think you need to worry about Luke Shipley, Ms. Carrera. If we don't find a smokin' gun with his prints on it—or smokin' gas can in this instance—he'll be fine. Crow Creek takes care of its own."

That statement both worried and reassured me. I turned from the detective and watched with surprise as a familiar white SUV pulled up the drive to park beside the judge's

155

black rental. Evie. And Maybelle. I shouldn't have been surprised to see them here. Actually, I'd half expected them to have already been here, trying to insert themselves into the search proceedings.

"Kay!"

Evie shouted and waved. Maybelle stayed by the vehicle, taking in the scene while the younger woman jogged up to the detective and started peppering him with questions. I made my way down to Maybelle. As I reached their SUV, I saw that she'd been looking down the driveway, watching a brown delivery truck coming toward the house.

"Gus said the UPS guy comes here all the time. Regularly. Several times a week," I remembered out loud.

"Delivering? Or picking up?" Maybelle strode forward as the delivery truck came to a stop behind our line of vehicles.

I followed her. "It's not like Kent Banner would be sending drug packages via UPS. Postal companies are pretty good at catching shipped drugs. Banner wouldn't be so stupid."

But the ghost had been holding a box, handing it off to someone. It *had* to be significant somehow.

The delivery man appeared, holding a package, frowning as he took in all the police activity. "What happened?"

Maybelle reached up for the package. "The resident died. The barn burned. If you've got something for Kent Banner, I'll take it and give it to the detective. He's got a warrant."

The delivery man's eyes widened. "Seriously? That sucks. The guy that lived here was nice."

He was the only one I'd heard voice that sentiment. I guessed even drug-dealing jerks could be polite to a few select people.

Maybelle took the box and we stood there, waiting until the UPS man was heading back down the driveway before examining it. The parcel was smaller than a shoe box, but the same shape. From the way Maybelle was hefting it, the box didn't weigh much. Leaning over her shoulder, I looked at the label.

It was addressed to White Light Pharmaceuticals, in the care of Kent Banner. The sender was KLP Medical Supplies.

Maybelle snorted. "White Light Pharmaceuticals. Fancy company name for a drug dealer."

"I wonder what he'd be buying from a medical supply company?" I mused.

"Let's see."

I gasped as she ripped open the package, using her fingernail to slice the tape sealing the box.

"Better to ask for forgiveness than permission," she commented cheerfully. "Bruce isn't going to throw me in jail for opening this up. He'd open it up anyway. I'm just saving him a step."

I didn't think this sort of thing would fly with the detectives I knew, but Crow Creek wasn't Locust Point. Peering over Maybelle's shoulder once more, I looked into the box.

It held two dozen empty pill bottles. One more confirmation that the rumors about Kent Banner were correct and he had, in fact, been packaging drugs for shipment here at the old Shipley farm.

CHAPTER 11

"I don't understand," Madison fussed. "Who would set Luke up like that? It's wrong. And it's not his fault if he hurt that other man."

"I feel bad for Luke, too. I don't think he murdered that man in cold blood, but he did admit to hitting him in the head with a hoof stand."

"The guy had a gun, and Luke was unarmed. He was defending himself," she interjected.

"True, but Luke was trespassing. Imagine if you lived in the middle of nowhere and found a stranger nosing around your barn and stables. There were better ways for Luke to handle the issue than hitting the man." I saw the frustration on Madison's face and reached out to touch her shoulder. "He has a lawyer. He hasn't been charged with the murder or the arson. The case is still open as far as the detective is concerned. You have to have faith in the system."

It was hard for me to say that when I didn't always have faith in the system. Madison's face fell, and I realized she was having the same thoughts that I was.

"The evidence is shaky," I reassured her. "Right now, there

isn't enough to accuse him of murder or arson. His lawyer can argue self-defense. Luke himself has no idea how badly he injured the man. It could have been a minor scrape, just enough for Luke to get away. When the coroner's report comes in, that might lead them to dropping the assault charges entirely."

She nodded. "It's just...Peony. I think about her and how unfair her sentence was. My dad is a judge. I *should* have faith in the system. But I see how politics, power, money, and social pressure have sway in a justice system that is supposed to be blind."

"I know. I think about Peony as well, but this situation is different. Peony was knowingly breaking the law; she just didn't intend for Holt to die. Luke at worst was committing a misdemeanor, and I even doubt that since there were no posted signs, and he'd never been notified not to trespass. The man who died had shot at someone before, and he had fired a shotgun as he was confronting Luke. I'm no lawyer, but if I was a jury, I'd say Luke had good reason to fear for his life, and that hitting the man with whatever he could grab nearby so he could get away wasn't a crime."

She nodded. "Okay. I'm going to try to have faith in the system, but only because you're in Luke's corner, Kay. I know you did everything you could to help Peony, and I know you'll do the same for Luke."

I was the one who'd talked Peony into turning herself in, and I still carried guilt over that. As for Luke...well, hopefully Detective Burnside was on the same path as me as far as a likely murder suspect. And if not, hopefully I could manage to set him on that path.

We finished getting ready for dinner, then headed downstairs to where Henry and Judge Beck were already at our dining table, ordering drinks and appetizers.

"I'm starving, and I promised Red I'd meet him out on the

slopes at six. He's going to teach me to do a 50-50," Madison told me as we made our way to the table.

I shook my finger at her. "Don't you dare rub your brother's face in it if you manage to master that thing. The poor kid just boarded the half-pipe without falling this afternoon."

Madison rolled her eyes. "Fine. But if he's not able to do the rails by the time we leave, I'm totally going to make fun of him."

Sibling rivalry. It was something I absolutely didn't understand. Madison and Henry loved each other, but one-on-one, they were sometimes so insensitive with their teasing.

"Be nice to your brother, or I'll make sure Red is teaching him the rest of the week and not you."

Her eyes shot wide. It made me laugh to think that a few days ago, she'd been lamenting how she had Red instructing her instead of Luke. It was odd that her competitive streak had finally won out over romance. Either that, or she was discovering the very different sort of attraction a young man such as Red could hold.

"Okay, I won't say a thing to Henry. Now let's eat. I swear I could eat a moose at this point."

Madison wasn't kidding. She and Henry each devoured an eight-ounce rib eye, a loaded baked potato, a salad, and a huge side of steamed broccoli and carrots with a creamy sauce. I shook my head, remembering what it was like to have a child's metabolism. Of course, I'd never been as tall as Madison either. The girl was just a hair shy of six feet at this point, and although it made her feel self-conscious, I absolutely was envious of her Amazonian height.

Henry was quickly catching up. He'd had a growth spurt the last few months, and I expected him to be outgrowing his clothes left and right this year, especially toward the fall when he entered high school. With Heather's height, *and*

Judge Beck's, I figured he would shoot up painfully fast. He might end up even taller than his father.

Madison reminded me so much of Judge Beck with her confidence and drive. Henry's confidence had a quieter, more harmonious bent. He was thoughtful, introspective, artistic.

But he still gobbled down his food and asked to be excused as soon as he could. It seemed he also had a meeting with his instructor.

"I bought them extra lessons for tonight," Judge Beck confessed once both the kids had raced off to the room to get their gear. "They're having such a good time, and I can tell they've got some sort of competition going on over who can master more of the terrain park features."

"They do." I shook my head. "I told Madison not to rub it in Henry's face, though. She's older, and she seems to be catching on quicker."

"He's used to it. And don't discount Henry. Once he gets the hang of something, he learns fast, where Madison tends to learn on a steadier trajectory."

"I just don't understand this sibling stuff," I confessed.

He laughed. "I do. My sister was a pain in the butt. I was always trying to keep up, to best her. I don't think I'd be the success I am today if it wasn't for her making fun of me and calling me a nerd for most of my life."

I knew he and his sister were close, and I envied him a sibling relationship. But I had close friends. I had him and the kids. And in some ways, that made up for the lack of living family members in my life.

"I'm going to be honest here and say I had an ulterior motive for buying the kids extra lessons." The judge's eyes met mine, and I saw something vulnerable in his gaze. "I wanted to spend some time alone with you. And we *did* make that deal about champagne and the hot tub."

My mind went blank for a split second, then I realized he was talking about our bet as we'd raced to the old Shipley farm that first night here. I had picked up a bottle of champagne the next day, but we'd ended up in the hot tub together, kids and all, so breaking out the bubbly had felt wrong.

"Absolutely. I promised, and I intend to deliver." I thought about what I'd just said and felt horribly flustered. Was that flirty? I hadn't meant it to be flirty. Or maybe I had.

He grinned, as if he caught the double meaning and approved. "Good. Let's go get our swimsuits on, and I'll meet you at the hot tub."

I took a quick sip of my coffee and rose. As I walked through the dining room, I swore I could feel Judge Beck's gaze on me. Where was this all going? For Pete's sake, I was a grown, mature woman. I *knew* where this was going, but even at sixty it gave me a nervous sort of anxiety. Did I want this…whatever *this* was? Part of me did, but another part of me was wracked with guilt and fear that any shift in my relationship with Judge Beck, anything that moved us from just friends to more, was going to end in disaster.

Madison had said there was no getting rid of her and Henry. Judge Beck and Heather were getting a divorce, and the kids still loved them both, but I hadn't even known them a year. Was that enough to solidify our bond? Because as much as it would kill me to eventually lose Judge Beck as a friend, and as something *more*, it would destroy me to lose Henry and Madison.

Up in our suite, I changed into the only swimsuit I'd brought. I'd purchased it last year when I'd fixed the hot tub because every suit I'd owned had practically been dry-rotted at that point. Daisy had talked me into an athletic one-piece with a scoop neck, and a back that was open practically to my rear in a ruby-red that I agreed was very flattering. I draped a gauzy floral wrap over the suit, then grabbed one of the towels and headed out, wondering where the heck Judge Beck was. He'd come back to the room right behind me, but there was no sign of him in the common area of our suite, and his bedroom door was closed. Deciding not to wait, I headed for the patio and our private hot tub.

I shivered in the sudden cold as I opened the door. The sky was dark, the stars so much brighter than they were at home, even with the faint golden glow of the lodge lights and those from the ski slope. Hurrying across the patio, I was practically on top of the stone platform that held the hot tub before I truly saw what was before me.

The only lights he'd turned on were the ones in the tub, which meant the stars were all the more brilliant. Soft music played from some hidden speakers. Etta James, I realized with a faint smile. An ice bucket on a stand was next to the hot tub and an open bottle of champagne inside, as well as two glasses that I assumed were plastic.

As I approached, Judge Beck stood, looking like Poseidon rising from the ocean. I jerked to a stop, gaping like a total fool. The water sheeted off his shoulders and chest. The moonlight glinted on the silvery strands in his dark-blond hair.

I swear my heart skipped a beat, as clichéd as that sounded.

"Kay. Get in here before you freeze to death."

Suddenly I realized I was standing in a bathing suit and a filmy wrap, holding a towel. And yes, I was freezing. I raced over to the hot tub, shivering like crazy as I hung my towel and wrap on the hooks. Then I quickly climbed the steps and eased myself into the blessed warmth.

"I didn't say anything the other night, but I like that swimsuit," Judge Beck told me.

"It's the same one I had all last summer," I replied, practicality forming my thoughts and words before I could come up with something flirty to say.

"Well, I still like it. Sit. I'll get you some champagne."

I almost plopped down on the far side of the hot tub, but some long rusty part of my brain finally engaged, and I made my way to sit next to him. He stood again and leaned over the edge of the hot tub to fill both glasses with champagne, passing one to me and settling in so close his arm brushed mine as he sat.

"Thank you." I sipped my champagne. "I've got something to confess, and it's probably a good time to do it since you're fed, relaxed, and drinking."

"Go ahead." He held his glass as if he weren't sure whether to drink it or to put it back.

I took another sip of my champagne. "I gave Luke Shipley a ride home from the jail. He confessed to going up to the farm to confront Kent Banner about his buying the place. Kent shot at him. They argued. Luke said he was worried the guy would shoot him, so he grabbed whatever was handy and whacked him in the head, taking the opportunity to run and get the heck out of there."

The judge let out a long breath. "Do they think he killed the man? Do *you* think he killed the man?"

I shook my head. "Not unless it was accidental. But then why was the body found in the barn instead of outside the stables? And who set the fire?"

"Could Luke be lying in hopes of a lesser charge? I'm assuming it was his badge at the scene, and that's what led the cops there. Smart criminals often realize a partial truth makes them seem genuine in the eyes of a jury, so they'll confess to some of the crime, but not the big-ticket items. Maybe he stayed after hitting the guy, panicked when he realized what happened, then dragged the body into the barn and set fire to it to cover everything up?"

"Even in the dark, the deputy and the firefighters would have noticed a huge smear of blood leading from the stables to the barn. And the badge was a fake, planted there to turn the attention toward Luke. It didn't have any lift stickers on it, and it was missing the pika sticker Madison stuck on it our first night here. Luke showed me his badge. He's got it. That one was a fake."

The judge sipped his champagne, trying and failing to hide a smile behind the glass. "You've spent more time sleuthing this vacation than skiing."

"In my defense, I can hardly ski for eight to ten hours a day. And I like sleuthing. I'm sorry a man died, that a barn burned, and that a young man I think is innocent is a suspect in these crimes, but in spite of that, I'm enjoying trying to get to the bottom of this mystery."

"Okay, Daphne," he teased.

"Velma," I corrected him. "Only with better vision."

He chuckled. "I've got something to confess as well."

I pivoted to face him. "Don't tell me you gave someone a lift home from the jail as well."

"No, nothing like that." He turned slightly also, his leg briefly brushing mine with the motion. "I was so worried you weren't going to have a good time on this vacation. I knew you hadn't skied in a long time, and I kept having these nightmares of you hating it or falling and ending up in the hospital with a broken leg. You'd have a miserable time, declare this the worst vacation ever, and regret that you agreed to come with me—us."

My heart twisted and before I could stop myself, I'd reached out and put my hand on his arm. "Surely you know me better than that. Even if I discovered I suddenly hate skiing, I'm the type of person who can always find something interesting to do. The town is adorable. There are a ton of activities. I could always go into Aspen and explore if I wanted or even sit in the café with a book and watch everyone on the slopes. I managed to find a mystery to stick my nose into, for Pete's sake."

He smiled. "I know. I just wanted everything to be perfect. It's our first vacation together, and I wanted you to love it."

I kept my hand on his arm. "I do love it. I'm having so much fun. I can't remember when I've felt as energized and relaxed all at the same time. This has been an amazing trip so far."

I shifted to face forward again, sliding my hand down his arm and under the water as I turned. His fingers captured mine, and he tugged so our shoulders touched.

"Do you know what I did this morning?" I asked, suddenly nervous about our proximity. "I skied a mogul field. And I didn't fall once. I've never been able to do that before. I was absolutely terrified, but I took a chance, and I'm so glad I did. Some things are worth facing your fear for, I've learned."

I realized that applied to a lot more than skiing, but *some* things were scarier than moguls. It would be worth it. It would be so worth it. I just had to take a chance, face my fears, and be willing to potentially suffer embarrassment and a broken heart as opposed to a broken leg.

"It's not just the skiing, the sleuthing, and the beauty of nature that have made this vacation so incredible," I continued. "I'm happy being with you...and the kids. Thank you for inviting me. Thank you for including me."

I leaned my head on his shoulder. His fingers tightened on mine for an instant, then he let go of my hand to tentatively snake his arm around my waist. My breath caught. With a quick sip of my champagne, I relaxed against him, feeling as if we'd crossed a bridge into new territory.

"You're part of our family, Kay," the judge's voice rumbled

warm and low. "I can't imagine experiencing something like this without you."

I sighed. Then I just enjoyed it all. We sat in silence, my head on his shoulder, his arm around me, his hand on my waist. Each time I lifted my glass to take a sip of champagne, my arm would brush against his side. I hadn't felt this tingly, this alive in…well, in a long time.

"Do you want more champagne?" he asked when my glass was empty.

"No, I'm good." I was good. Besides, him pouring more champagne in my glass would involve the both of us moving away from each other, and I didn't want to break the spell.

We stayed that way until the lights on the terrain park and ski slopes flickered the warning that the chair lift would soon shut down and those still out would need to use the J-bar lift. I expected Judge Beck to pull away, for our hot tub time to end. He wouldn't want the kids to come back in and find us snuggled up together drinking champagne.

The man didn't budge. Actually, his hand tightened on my waist, as if he feared *I'd* be the one who moved away. Then he sighed and slid his hand along my back as he shifted on the seat.

"Well, *I'm* having more."

He twisted to reach the bottle, and I went ahead and held out my glass. "Since you've got that bottle handy…."

He filled both our glasses, put the bottle back into the ice, then settled once more in the hot tub.

"I'm proud of you for tackling the moguls." He toasted me with his glass. "The kids want to head in early tomorrow. Maybe we can ski a few slopes together before your lesson."

Drat. I wanted to, but Eric—aka The Badge Guy—would be opening the gift shop tomorrow morning and I'd hoped to talk to him before heading to the slopes. I bit my lip, wondering if I could put it off and come back at noon instead. There really wasn't any rush, but my curiosity was gnawing away at me. I had a feeling Eric was key to finding out who planted that badge. Plus, I wanted to get a good look at Rocky's truck.

"I'd love that. If not before my lessons, then after." I smiled up at him. "I've got a few things I wanted to do tomorrow morning, and I'm not sure if they'll wait or not."

"Sleuthing?" His eyebrows rose.

"Sleuthing," I confirmed. "Oh! I forgot to tell you that I went out to the farm again this afternoon. Detective Burnside had his warrant, and he was there with some officers searching the premises. Unfortunately, I doubt I'm getting my pen back."

He shook his head, a puzzled expression on his face.

"The UPS man showed up while I was talking to Evie and Maybelle," I continued. "Remember how Gus said Kent Banner must have gotten a lot of deliveries because the UPS truck was there several times a week?"

"No." The judge still looked perplexed. "I don't think you told me that. Who's Gus? Isn't that your ski instructor?"

"Yes, he is." I waved that fact away. "The UPS driver handed us a package and Maybelle opened it." I held my hand up at the protest ready to come out of his mouth. "It was open before I could stop her. Anyway, the box held a bunch of empty pill bottles. It was from a place called KLP Medical Supplies, and it was addressed to a White Light Pharmaceuticals in the care of Kent Banner. I guess that proves he was involved in some sort of drug distribution. Hopefully, the murder was tied to his illegal business dealings, and Luke will be off the hook."

This time his arm came around my shoulder. "Is this really about Luke, or is it about Peony? I know you still feel guilty about what happened, and how her plea bargain didn't end up with the sentence everyone thought she'd get."

I laughed, scooting closer to him. "Are you a judge or a psychologist? You're one-hundred-percent right, but that still doesn't mean I don't care about someone who I think is innocent possibly being brought up on murder charges."

"We both feel very strongly about justice, even though we don't always agree about the definition of that word," he mused.

"We do." I thought once more about all the other things we had in common. I admired him. I respected him. And I wasn't quite ready to admit to any stronger emotions than that, even if my practical mind knew I felt them.

"Drink up." His fingers rubbed along my shoulder. "Let's get out of this hot tub before we wrinkle up into a pair of raisins."

I obeyed, handing the judge my glass when I'd finished. He stashed both glasses in the ice bucket with the champagne bottle and got out of the hot tub, standing there in the freezing cold to help me out and wrap me in a towel before turning to grab one for himself. He took my elbow as I shivered my way into the room.

"Going...to...change...." I chattered as I dashed to the bedroom. Cold wasn't sexy, and suddenly I wanted to be sexy even if that meant fleece pajamas and fluffy slippers when it came to my choice of attire.

When I came out, the judge had also changed into his pajamas and was holding his laptop as he sat at the table.

"What are you doing?" I gave my hair one last quick rub with the towel and watched the judge fire up his computer. Was he going to work? After the flirty stuff in the hot tub, he was going to *work*?

"I thought we'd check out a few things, such as that White Light Pharmaceuticals the package was addressed to." He typed in his password.

I pulled a chair up next to him. "I figured it was a fake

name, something Banner made up so the medical supply company wouldn't get suspicious shipping dozens of empty pill bottles to an individual."

"Well, KLP Medical Supplies is legit." The judge angled the laptop so I could better see the screen. "There aren't any restrictions on most of what they're selling. Yes, they offer bulk orders of things like those empty pill bottles, but they also sell mobility devices, bed pans, and stuff like that."

"Detective Burnside can always subpoena their records to determine what Kent Banner purchased, the quantities, and when," I mused. "Although he might not bother with the drug angle if he finds further proof that points toward Luke Shipley as the killer."

The judge's fingers flew over the keyboard, then he hit the enter key. His eyebrows shot up, and he laughed.

"Kay? You've got to see this." He pivoted the laptop once more. "Kent Banner wasn't dealing drugs—at least not the drugs everyone thought."

On the screen was a flashy website for White Light Pharmaceuticals. The company promised low-cost prescription drugs as well as "proven" herbal remedies. Had that been what the pill bottles were for? What the dehydrator was for? What the leafy stuff drying on the tables in the barn was for? It seemed Kent Banner had been somehow procuring pills from other countries and re-selling them, as well as producing herbal supplements, that may or may not have been legitimate, in the treatment of various ailments.

It wasn't aboveboard, but it wasn't mixing heroin with baking soda and shipping the bricks on down the distribution chain. No wonder the man had wanted his privacy. Outside of Cheryl cutting through the back forty and Luke harassing him about offering to buy the place, the old Shipley farm had been perfect. The only person regularly getting within a quarter mile of the house was the UPS driver.

"Wanna bet Mr. Banner's business has had a few brushes with the law in the past?" the judge asked, his eyes twinkling. "I'll bet someone with a talent for digging around the internet could discover all sorts of things in his background."

I grinned, reaching for my own laptop. "You don't mind?" This was hardly the finish to the champagne and hot tub evening he must have had in mind, but then again, I didn't think either of us were quite ready to go racing down that path—at least tonight.

"Not at all. I love watching you work."

My head jerked up, and I eyed him, more than a little suspicious at his tone. "You've got some brief or motion you need to work on, don't you?"

He hid a smile. "Well, if you're going to do some research, I might as well get in a little work myself."

The kids would be snowboarding for a while longer. We had the suite all to ourselves. The pair of us were our pajamas, our hair still wet. I pulled a chair over close to him—so close I could feel the warmth from his skin as I sat down.

The time we'd spent working together at my dining room table had solidified our relationship, given it a sturdy foundation of respect and professional admiration. As odd as it seemed, this felt right. We'd been taking small steps forward, exploring what our friendship might become, but anchoring that unknown in the familiar like this gave me a sense that it would all be fine. I hoped romance was in our future. But in the meantime, the judge and I had this. We both shared a love for his children, and between the two of us, we had this.

Turning on my laptop, I shot him a quick smile, scooted my chair even closer, and got to work.

CHAPTER 12

*K*ent Banner might not have been involved in a heroin ring, but he was absolutely a drug dealer. I found links that made me suspect he'd been running this business of his under various names for over a decade. White Light Pharmaceuticals had appeared on the scene six months ago, but before then, there had been at least twelve other internet-based companies selling the same products and all leading back to Kent Banner via a convoluted trail.

The kids had returned from the slopes and gone to bed. Judge Beck had turned in half an hour ago, but I still sat at the table in my pajamas, the lights dimmed as I tapped away at my keyboard.

Every time complaints had mounted to the point where Kent Banner's business might draw the attention of various law enforcement or regulatory agencies, the man wiped it out and created a new one. He'd lived various places in Colorado and Nevada, but the internet scam he was running was so hidden behind shell company names, overseas registrations, and firewalls that it would have taken someone dedicated to follow the breadcrumbs to him.

And so far, no one had been dedicated enough to care about a small-time peddler of non-FDA approved medicines. Banner had repackaged sketchy pharmaceuticals that he seemed to have bought in bulk from Asia and South America as well as selling herbal cure-alls. Judging by his financials, the man wasn't pulling in millions, but he was turning a steady profit of two to three hundred thousand a year.

And looking at the "reviews" his various companies had accumulated, his customers either believed in the snake oil he was selling or were too embarrassed they'd been had to voice more than a mild complaint. There were a few civil suits here and there, but they'd been dropped because either Banner had shuttered his company and the plaintiffs lacked the funds to dig deep enough to ferret out the company owner, or they simply lacked the funds to push the suit forward.

The guy was a dirt bag, and part of me felt he'd gotten what he deserved. I remembered how terribly expensive Eli's medicines had been, how the accident and the following ten years of health care had eaten up every bit of our retirement savings. We'd been lucky to have had the money. Some weren't so lucky. I hated Kent Banner for preying on those people, for taking advantage of their desperation. Who knew what sort of stuff he'd been shipping to his customers in those pill bottles? Herbal remedies aside, the drugs he'd gotten from overseas could have held anything. How many people had worsened, thinking they were merely taking a lesser-priced alternative to what their doctor had prescribed? How many had died because the pills they thought managed their health condition contained nothing but baking soda and sugar?

Then I thought about the fire, about Luke Shipley's future on the line, about Banner pulling out a gun during their argument, about Banner shooting at Cheryl as she cut across his property. The world might be a better place without Kent Banner in it, but there still was a killer out there that needed to face justice.

And I was doubly convinced that killer wasn't Luke Shipley.

I downloaded screenshots and sent them to Detective Burnside as well as to my own phone. I took notes, filling one of the pads the lodge had kindly provided for us. Then at about three in the morning, I finally dragged myself off to bed.

* * *

Four hours later, Madison woke me up with a mug of coffee and a plate of sliced fruit. "Are you feeling all right? You don't usually sleep this soundly."

I sat up, rubbing the crust from my eyes. "I got caught up in something and didn't get to bed until late. Thanks for waking me. And thanks for the coffee."

Taking the mug from her, I inhaled deeply, then sipped. Madison put the plate of food on the nightstand and stood by the bed.

"Are you coming with us? Dad said if you want to sleep in a bit more, he can come back later in the morning or around lunch time to pick you up."

The gift shop opened at eight and there were a few other things I wanted to do before strapping on my skis, but this was our vacation, and I was supposed to have a lesson at ten o'clock with Gus.

I swung my feet out of bed, knowing that I'd be running it close, but if I hustled, I might be able to be there in time for my lesson.

"You guys go ahead," I told Madison. "I'll grab an Uber." I

probably should update Evie anyway. This would give me the perfect opportunity.

A shower and two cups of coffee later, I was heading down to the lobby and out the front door. The lodge van was parked over to the side of the main building. The red truck with the logo on the driver's door was next to it.

Cheryl had said Rocky wouldn't let anyone else drive this truck. It had to have been him the judge and I had seen driving down the road right before we'd skied over to the old Shipley farm and seen the fire. Maybe there was another red truck like this in Crow Creek with a logo on the door, but I doubted it. Maybe Rocky had been on that road right after the fire was set for innocent reasons, but that road only led to Cheryl's place and the old Shipley Farm. Besides, Rocky must have seen the smoke coming from the barn as he drove past. Why hadn't he called it in? At the very least, he was a witness. At worst, he was a murderer.

He wanted to use the trails on the farm, and I was willing to bet Banner would have said a very vehement "no" to that proposal. Maybe they argued, just as Banner and Luke had done. Maybe Banner had pulled his gun just as he'd done with so many other people.

Maybe the blow Luke had struck hadn't been the only one, and instead of running, Rocky had started the fire to cover it up.

Then he'd come back later and thrown a fake badge down near the barn to lead police in a different direction. Whether he intended Luke to go down for murder or just meant to muddy the waters was something I was still pondering.

And all this was conjecture. I had some clues, but they were just as damning to Cheryl and Luke as they were to Rocky—maybe more so.

"Do you need a lift somewhere?"

I turned to see a man about my age with bushy silver

eyebrows, an equally bushy silver walrus mustache, and a jacket with the lodge logo.

"Just let them know at the front desk," he continued. "I'm free until nine-thirty when I need to take the family in one-oh-five to the airport."

"I won't need a ride, but I had a question." I turned slightly and pointed to the red pick-up. "Does anyone besides Rocky drive this?"

He tilted his head as he regarded me with curiosity. "No. Well, except for me when I'm taking it to get cleaned."

"How often do you have it cleaned?" I tried to peer through the passenger window without looking like I was trying to peer through the passenger window.

He chuckled. "Usually once a week except for spring when it gets muddy around here, or if Mr. Rocky hits a skunk or spills something." He wrinkled his nose, bunching up the mustache. "I've had to clean it twice this week already. Thing reeked of gasoline."

Jackpot. "When did you notice the truck smelled of gasoline?"

"Three days ago." The mustache wiggled. "Actually four. That night I parked the van after an airport run and noticed the smell even with the doors closed. I went in and asked Rocky if he wanted me to clean it the next morning when I did the van."

"Why would his truck smell like gasoline?" I asked, thinking there was one reason I knew of—he'd used it to start a fire and spilled some on himself in the process.

The man shrugged. "People fill up gas cans in the winter for snowmobiles and four wheelers. I figured he spilled some on himself."

It sounded reasonable until the gasoline smell coincided with the judge and I seeing the truck in the area right after the fire had been set.

I thanked the man and headed back to the lodge, eyeing my phone for the time. The gift shop was just opening when I arrived. Eric, aka The Badge Guy, held a box in one hand and a cup of coffee in the other. He raised the box when he saw me approach.

"We've got more stickers in," he announced. "Your daughter was the one who liked the pika stickers, right? Let her know if she wants more to come see me."

"Actually, I had a few questions about the badge system."

He put the box down and motioned for me to follow him to the kiosk. "Sure. Is there a problem with yours? Sometimes the barcodes get scratched, and they won't scan."

"No, mine is fine. This is more about procedure and access and..." I pulled my phone out and pulled up the picture of the badge I'd found by the barn. "Basically, what can you tell me about this badge?"

He squinted at the picture. "It's either new, or the person who had it hadn't gone skiing yet. There aren't any lift stickers." He stepped behind the kiosk, typed on the keyboard, then looked at the picture again. "That's a staff badge. The number is the new batch, so it would have been assigned in the last few months. Actually, with that number, I'd say this week since I tend to just pull them from the box in numerical order. The number, plus the lack of lift stickers...I'd say it was a staff badge printed up within the last few days."

"Not a year ago?" I asked, just to be sure.

He laughed. "Not with that number. And not unless it was a staff member who didn't need to be on the slopes a lot, like someone from housekeeping or the front desk. Here." He typed on the keyboard again. "Let me see who it belongs to."

I waited and watched him frown as the data came up.

"Luke Shipley. But...this can't be right."

"What can't be right?" I prodded.

"It says the badge was issued last year, but that would be

impossible for this badge number. Plus, where are the lift stickers? Even if they'd been damaged, there should be some residue and some bits of the stickers still attached. That glue is like cement." He typed something else, then slowly shook his head. "This says the badge Luke has now was just issued three days ago, but that badge number is from a batch we got over a year ago. If Luke got a replacement badge, the number would be closer to the one in your picture, not this."

"Who has the authority to change record history? Who can backdate a badge and alter the issue date of a current one?"

"Not me, that's for sure." He shook his head again. "I can add a record as a correction, but not alter the history. You never want to alter history in a database. It's important to have a record of every change."

"You, Cheryl, and Rocky are the only ones with access to the system, right?"

He nodded. "Yeah. I don't have the ability to add users or assign security levels. Rocky does. I'm assuming Cheryl does as well, but I'm not positive."

"Can you get in to see what security level each user has?" I asked.

He typed a bit, then leaned back. "I've got level 3, so I can assign badges, add a record to change a badge, and suspend or delete a badge's access. Cheryl has level 2, so she can do all that plus add level 3 users. Rocky has level 1, and I'm not sure what extras that allows."

Rocky. But I wasn't ready to completely rule out Cheryl at this point.

"Whose username is on the records for Luke's badges? Both the one he supposedly got last year, and the one he supposedly just got this week?" I asked.

Eric flipped back to the other screens, then paled. "Me. But it wasn't me. I didn't do this. I don't even have access to do this." He turned to me, eyes pleading. "Ms. Carrera, I've got no idea what's going on here, but I didn't change this system. Someone's trying to set me up. And it looks like someone's trying to set Luke up for something as well."

Someone indeed was trying to set Luke up, and throw Eric under the bus if the deception was detected. Luckily, that someone wasn't as smart as they thought they were.

"Can you keep quiet about this?" I asked Eric. "Don't tell anyone. I'm going to meet with Detective Burnside and let him know what you told me, and he'll probably be by later today to talk to you, but until then, please keep this all to yourself."

Eric nodded, logging off the computer with sweaty hands. "Do you think I need to call a lawyer?"

"Not now. Probably not in the near future, either."

But someone else will, I thought as I left the gift shop and pulled out my phone to e-mail everything I'd found out to Detective Burnside, planning to call Evie for a ride once I was done.

CHAPTER 13

*B*efore I could even dial Evie, I saw Judge Beck walking through the front door of the lodge, Detective Burnside beside him. The pair were chatting as though they were old friends, which surprised me since the judge hadn't met the detective to my knowledge. I hesitated, then stuck my phone back into my pocket.

"Ms. Carrera." The detective bowed. "I met your friend in the parking lot, and we've had a nice conversation about the information you discovered as well as your theories on my case."

He didn't seem to be irritated at my meddling, but I felt more than a little embarrassed. The detective was competent, and absolutely able to investigate this on his own, but here I was sticking my nose into everything as if I'd been assigned to the investigation. Maybe I should have just minded my own business and stuck with the ski slopes.

"I'm sorry. I hope I'm not interfering with your case." I winced, thinking that I'd just sent him a detailed, and enthusiastic, e-mail about the badge records as well as what the van driver had said about Rocky's truck smelling of gasoline.

"Not at all." He gestured for the judge and me to sit at a little conversational area in the lobby. "One thing you learn growing up in Crow Creek is to work with the local busybodies instead of fighting against 'em. People know some pretty useful things, and when a detective is appreciative, then people are happy to share."

I wasn't sure how I felt about being lumped in with the town busybodies, but in all honesty, the label wasn't wrong.

"I'm glad you found that badge, because it told me a lot of things," Detective Burnside went on. "Deputy Raine, the fire marshal, and I went over that crime scene practically on hands and knees right at sunup. We'd searched it the night before after the fire was out using some high-powered lights, but it's always better to double check once daylight comes, don't you think?"

I nodded. "And you didn't find a badge."

"Nope. We found some blood out near one of the stable stalls, including some bloody fingerprints—all of which, blood and prints both, were Kent Banner's."

"That supports what Luke said about where they were when he hit him," I mused.

"Yep. But the body was found inside the barn. Mind you, sometimes fatal head wounds take a little while. We've sadly discovered that a few times with skiers. Still, I found it mighty interesting that Luke had been there close to the time of the actual murder, and that a badge pointing to him—one in plain sight that three trained investigators missed during two sweeps of the scene—was found."

"The killer knew Luke was there!" I exclaimed. "Luke parked around the side of the barn, and he was probably so focused on getting out of there without getting shot that he didn't notice the other vehicle."

The detective grinned. "You catch on quick, Ms. Carrera. That stuff about the badge not having stickers on it? I found that peculiar as well, and the melt patterns didn't jive according to the expert I consulted. Looked more like someone took a grill lighter to the badge and the lanyard than if it had been in a fire. None of the important parts of the barcode or number were gone—carefully preserved so it was easy to identify who it was issued to. The lanyard was burned off and blackened, but the clip attaching it to the badge was bright and shiny, without so much as a smudge of soot on it."

"I didn't notice that." I wished we had a Detective Burnside in Locust Point because discussing the case with a fellow investigator was exciting.

"We questioned Luke Shipley and when he confessed, we booked him on an assault charge that the prosecutor may decide to drop now that the official coroner results are in." Detective Burnside leaned forward, as if imparting a valuable secret. "That head wound? There wasn't just one, there were two. First one wasn't too bad, and that wound matched that hoof stand. The second one was pretty serious, and it matched a hammer we found under one of the melted plastic tables inside the barn."

"So, Kent Banner was okay when Luke left, minus a bit of blood loss," the judge said. "Soon after that, he went into the barn, I guess to check on those leaves he was drying for his fake medicines. There he encountered someone else who hit him with a hammer, then started the fire?"

The detective nodded. "I circled back after Rocky looked the badge up in the system and interviewed the lodge staff, asking questions about Luke, but also asking lots of questions about who was where at the night of the fire. Rocky and Cheryl were making the rounds in the dining area, and it looked like everyone had an alibi except Luke. Then Heather, the young lady working the front desk that night, remembered that Rocky got a call around four-thirty that had him worked up. He left, and she didn't see him again until after six-thirty. By then, Cheryl had rushed out to respond to the fire call." The detective held up a finger to hold off my comment. "Two of the guests saw Rocky coming back closer to six. One approached him to ask a question about check out times and told me that Rocky smelled of gasoline."

"The lodge van driver told me his truck smelled like gasoline as well," I offered. "He took the truck in the next day to clean it up and try to get the smell out."

The detective nodded. "But there was no gas can in the truck or in the bed. It's pretty common around here to go fill up a can of gas for your snowmobile or four-wheeler, and it's also pretty common to spill a little on your hands, but no one saw Rocky unloading a can of gas when he came back, and there wasn't any in the truck, according to witnesses."

"Because he left the can at the barn to burn up," I finished.

"Yep. He did. I doubt we'll find the clothes in his room since he probably ditched them days ago, but I do think we'll find some interesting e-mails and phone calls about that trail he's so hot to put in." The detective leaned back, a satisfied smile on his face. "No wonder you all took the wrong turn skiing that night. That trail is almost finished. It's not cheap putting in something like that, and Rocky is a determined man. He was having his trail no matter what."

"But the owner wouldn't have agreed unless Rocky was buying the land from him," I commented. "And Kent Banner was buying the farm. He wouldn't have wanted a bunch of tourist skiers that close to the farm."

"Witnesses had seen the lodge truck there a few times the past few months. Seems Rocky had started work on the new trail, assuming that the property would remain vacant and no one would know he hadn't gotten permission or compensated the owner. After all, the owner had never stepped foot on the property or in town, and as a stranger, none of the locals would bother to check if Rocky had gotten the okay or not."

"Then Kent Banner moved in," I mused.

"And instead of being a nice cooperative sort of guy, he takes to shooting at trespassers and defending his privacy and the property like he was running a drug operation out of there." Detective Burnside chuckled. "Which he kind of was. We found all his business records inside the house. We also found several grainy videos Kent Banner had taken of him and Rocky having words. Seems after shooting at Cheryl, Banner put up a few cheap cameras to monitor the barn and the driveway. There's no audio, but it's pretty clear the two aren't having a friendly discussion."

"Rocky was all set to open that trail. He told us it would be available for use in a few weeks," I commented.

"Things came together fast on this one, but I needed to wait for the coroner's report. And I needed to wait for access to some cell phone information. Normally that stuff takes forever, but I pulled in a few favors and was able to see that the four-thirty call Rocky received was from Kent Banner. Piecing together texts and voice mail messages, it looks like Rocky was trying to blackmail Banner into letting him use the land for the trail, telling him he was going to get him arrested for his illegal drug dealings."

"And Banner called his bluff?" Judge Beck asked.

"Probably. Unlicensed sales of herbal remedies and prescription drugs isn't legal, but it's not the sort of thing that's going to get a SWAT team breaking down your door. Banner had re-invented his business before. He must have known Rocky didn't really know what he was doing, and that he was safe."

"I'll bet he went out there to confront Banner and probably ended up facing the barrel of that shotgun, just like Luke had," I said. "And like Luke, Rocky grabbed whatever was at hand and hit the man."

"Then compounded his crime by setting the fire."

I sighed. "He'll probably claim self-defense." Which I understood in Luke's case, but not in Rocky's. He had been attempting to blackmail the man. He'd gone out there after an argument, looking for trouble.

"Hard to claim self-defense when the blow was in the back of the man's skull. Banner had turned his back on Rocky. Shotgun or not, that's looking like first-degree murder in my books." Detective Burnside shook his head. "The man might have lived if he'd gotten medical attention. It was smoke inhalation that did him in, even though the head wound was pretty bad."

"He wanted to kill him," I thought out loud.

"That's what I'm thinking. Now he might claim it was a heat-of-the-moment thing, but the blackmail and the nearly finished trail tell a different story. Banner dies, then the property stays vacant for another few years. New tenant moves in and probably assumes the land where the trail is isn't part of the property, or that maybe the owner leased it off, and Rocky's good."

"Or Luke buys the farm and needs the money, so he leases the land to Rocky," I added.

Detective Burnside shrugged. "Maybe. Course, if Luke's spending all his money defending himself on murder charges, then he can't very well buy the place, and Rocky doesn't even need to bother paying to lease the land. Too bad he didn't think far enough ahead to have that badge ready when he went out to confront Banner instead of having to go out the next day and plant the evidence."

At that moment, a scuffle by the deck doors drew my attention. Two uniformed officers were leading Rocky Forrest in handcuffs through the lobby.

"This is my cue to skedaddle," Detective Burnside said as he rose from his chair. "It was real nice meeting you folks. I hope you come back and visit us soon, although I can't guarantee another mystery for you to poke your nose into, Ms. Carrera."

I smiled up at him, rising as well. "Then I'll just have to come for the skiing and the natural beauty. It was good meeting you as well, Detective Burnside. You're a credit to your ancestors."

He dipped his head and joined the officers. Judge Beck stood by my side and watched as they led a silent, red-faced Rocky out the door and to the awaiting police car.

"I'm a bit disappointed," the judge said. "I really was hoping for one of those 'I'd have gotten away with it if it hadn't been for that meddling lady' speeches."

"I'm a busybody, not a meddling lady," I corrected, thinking that Detective Burnside had been doing just fine without this meddling lady sticking her nose into the case. But sleuthing on vacation had been fun, and I'd met some really interesting people. I'd need to call Evie and Maybelle and clue them in to this morning's happenings—although with the gossip network in this town, they probably already knew.

"Oh, no!" I glanced at the lobby clock in alarm. "My lesson! Poor Gus. I've stood him up."

"I took the liberty of canceling your morning lesson when I dropped the kids off at the slopes," Judge Beck told me. "I figured you'd be cutting it close at best, and most likely too far into your investigative work to be there at ten. Let's ski together instead, then grab lunch. I'll admit I've been a bit jealous of Gus getting to spend the morning with you every day this week."

Jealous. I doubted he'd really been jealous of the ski

instructor, but I did think he was honest about wishing he'd been the one spending that time with me instead.

"I'd love to ski with you. And have lunch." I held up a finger in warning. "But if we do any of the steep slopes or mogul fields, I might fall."

"Then I'll be there to pick you up," he promised. "Just don't knock me off the chair lift."

My heart did interesting things at the warmth in his eyes. "I won't. I think I've managed to master the chair lift."

He hesitated a second, then stepped close, draping an arm over my shoulder. I stepped into him to let him know I was okay with the gesture. I was more than okay. With a little nervous flutter in my chest, I put my arm around his waist.

"Ready?" he asked.

I took a deep breath, then smiled up at him. "Ready."

And I was. Ready, that is. Ready to ski and ready to face my other fears and take slow steps forward in the other areas of my life as well.

* * *

I HOPE you enjoyed Fire and Ice!

Book 11 in the Locust Point Mystery Series, Best in Breed, will be available next, so stay tuned and keep reading. —Libby

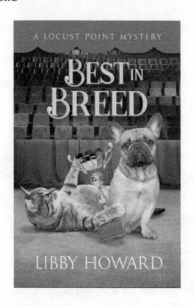

Locust Point Mystery Series:

The Tell All

Junkyard Man

Antique Secrets

Hometown Hero

A Literary Scandal

Root of All Evil

A Grave Situation

Last Supper

A Midnight Clear

Fire and Ice

Best in Breed

ACKNOWLEDGMENTS

Thanks to Lyndsey Lewellen for cover design and typography, and to Erin Zarro for copyediting. And special thanks to all my readers who patiently waited for this book. Read, knit, snuggle your Taco, and take a chance on love.

ABOUT THE AUTHOR

Libby Howard lives in a little house in the woods with her sons and two exuberant bloodhounds. She occasionally knits, occasionally bakes, and occasionally manages to do a load of laundry. Most of her writing (pre-COVID) was done in a bar where she could combine work with people-watching, a decent micro-brew, and a plate of Old Bay wings. This year, however, it's all about pajamas and the couch.

For more information:
libbyhowardbooks.com/

CPSIA information can be obtained
at www.ICGtesting.com
Printed in the USA
LVHW100543060223
738715LV00023B/151

9 781952 216374